MR MOON'S LAST CASE

Retired superintendent Reginald Moon is eccentric, tired of life and still believes in fairies. One night he sees a strange child-like figure leap from a bridge on to a moving goods-train, and having nothing better to do, decides to follow it. As he trails his quarry from farm to village to city, he begins to realize a fantastic truth.

Meanwhile in the dwarf village of Oakwood, the inquisitive Nameon has unearthed an ancient map and gone missing . . . Lost and confused in the human world, the dwarf's only aim is to return home as soon as possible. A delightful collection of characters help and hinder him, and all the time Mr Moon is getting closer.

Mr Moon's Last Case is original, funny and poignant. It is a modern fairy-tale and a detective story. Brian Patten has created an original and lasting fantasy with lovable and funny characters. The book has received a special award from the Mystery Writers of America Guild, and has been described by many reviewers as a potential classic.

Brian Patten has published numerous books of poetry and his work has been translated into many languages. He writes for both children and adults.

Brian Patten

MR MOON'S LAST CASE

Illustrated by Mark Southgate

PUFFIN BOOKS

PUFFIN BOOKS

Published by the Penguin Group
27 Wrights Lane, London w8 5tz, England
Viking Penguin Inc., 40 West 23rd Street, New York, New York 10010, USA
Penguin Books Australia Ltd, Ringwood, Victoria, Australia
Penguin Books Canada Ltd, 2801 John Street, Markham, Ontario, Canada l3r 1b4
Penguin Books (NZ) Ltd, 182–190 Wairau Road, Auckland 10, New Zealand

Penguin Books Ltd, Registered Offices: Harmondsworth, Middlesex, England

First published by George Allen & Unwin Ltd 1975
and subsequently by Unwin Hyman Ltd
Published in Puffin Books 1988
1 3 5 7 9 10 8 6 4 2

Made and printed in Great Britain by
Cox and Wyman Ltd, Reading, Berks
Filmset in Linotron Baskerville by
Rowland Phototypesetting Ltd,
Bury St Edmunds, Suffolk

FOR
LIZZY GRAHAM AND ELIZABETH HAMBLETT

AUTHOR'S NOTE
ABOUT THIS STORY

FICTIONAL stories, even the most fantastic, often have their starting point in true incidents. This is one such story.

Some years ago a young boy told a group of friends he had seen a leprechaun or some kind of goblin in a Liverpool park. Within a day his story had spread like wildfire through the city, and the park was besieged by over two thousand children, many of them playing truant. A sports match was cancelled, fights broke out, a first-aid tent doubled as a base for lost children, traffic round the park was thrown into chaos, and dozens of policemen and members of the St Johns Ambulance Brigade spent hours trying to cope with the situation.

The rumour persisted, and several weeks later came other reports. They were often bizarre. The creature had been found dead in a public toilet; it had been seen hiding in a cemetery. The last report was that the leprechaun was living on wasteland behind Otterspool Promenade, an area then strewn with oil drums and debris from the River Mersey. The summer passed, the excitement faded, and the creature was forgotten.

I often wondered what might have happened to the creature had it been real. Perhaps it was. Perhaps it believed our world was the unreal world, a fantastic fairy-tale in which it had got lost.

I

ONE bitterly cold winter's night some time in January the second mate of the *Irish Rose*, a passenger ship plying from Dublin to Brumble Head in Wales, noticed something peculiar about a lifeboat. On investigating he discovered curled up inside it a creature resembling a leprechaun. Of course Patrick O'Halligan did not think it was a leprechaun. He mistook it for a child, but such a strange-looking child that he did not wake it. Instead he hurried along to inform the captain of its existence. The boat had docked, and its few passengers disembarked about an hour before. It was drizzling and the mist was so thick it obscured anything over a distance of several yards.

O'Halligan rushed into the captain's cabin. 'There's a weird-looking child asleep in one of the lifeboats,' he said. Thinking the second mate drunk the captain ignored him, but when O'Halligan insisted that the child was real he went to look. Of course by then the lifeboat was empty.

Gavin Thomas, a night watchman employed by the North Wales Docks & Harbour Board was sitting dreaming of things long gone when he saw what he mistook for an alsatian's shadow dart between the landing stage and the boat sheds. He immediately telephoned to the dock-gates where the security guard, Dai Bevan, was reading a comic.

'There's a dog down here, a big one,' said Gavin Thomas.

'Is it tame?' asked Dai Bevan.

'I don't know,' said his friend.

Both men were rather timid and neither enjoyed the idea of searching for a large and probably vicious animal in dark sheds late on a filthy evening. For a while they simply talked over the telephone about what they should do, hoping in the meantime that the dog would go away. But eventually they decided they had better join forces to investigate.

They met half-way between the landing stage and the dock-gates in a customs shed long fallen into disuse.

'Have you seen it again?' asked the security guard.

'No,' said the night watchman.

The men peered through the gloom afraid that any sudden movement might bring them into contact with a raving dog. The shadow seen by the night watchman had already grown in both men's minds to absurd proportions. If it had been a foreign vessel docking at Brumble Head they would have assumed the shadow to be that of a tiger or some other unmanageable beast and informed the necessary authorities without delay. But as it was only the *Irish Rose* that bobbed harmlessly in the mist, and as the shadow was more likely to be that of a poodle than a tiger, the two men stood in the brightest and safest part of the customs shed resigned to dealing with the situation themselves.

Before they could decide on any plan of action, around the corner of the nothing-to-declare desk came the creature from the boat. When it saw the men it jerked to a halt, looked frantically for a means of escape, then darted off in a different direction.

'Good grief,' cried Dai Bevan, 'it's a child, not a dog.'

'And he's sick,' said Gavin Thomas.

'Sick! I'd say he was at death's door. Did you notice his face? I've never seen such a face. He looked terrified.'

'I wonder why?' asked the night watchman, suddenly thinking that perhaps the boy was being chased by the alsatian he had so vividly imagined. They followed after the small figure and saw it again only when it was climbing over the dock-gates out into the cobbled streets of Brumble Head.

Assuming a voice of authority, Dai Bevan said, 'I'd better phone the police then.'

Thus the first alarm was raised and the hunt was on for Nameon, one of the few dwarfs ever to visit the human world. He had come by accident and immediately upon arriving his sole ambition was to get back home.

2

POLICE Sergeant Watts was preparing to spend a quiet evening with his friend, ex-superintendent Reginald Moon, when he unexpectedly received a telephone call from Brumble Head Police Station. He listened with much agitation to the voice at the far end of the phone, for he was supposed to be off duty, and when the voice had finished he slammed down the receiver.

'There goes our quiet evening,' he said. 'The station has received a report about someone causing a disturbance down at the docks, and they want me to investigate. Are you well enough to come along?'

'Of course I am,' said Mr Moon. But he was not.

That afternoon Mr Moon had been forced against his will into visiting a doctor's surgery. He had been made to say 'arr' many times, and to cough and stick his tongue out, and to raise and lower his legs. He had been weighed and his weight checked against his previous weight. Finally, looking very solemn, the doctor had given him a sealed note to take to the hospital where he was to be X-rayed and, no doubt, prodded again. Mr Moon had not gone to the hospital. He disliked being prodded and he had no wish to know the content of the doctor's note.

'Of course I'm well enough,' he grunted. 'I'm well enough to do anything.'

And so Sergeant Watts went out to investigate, escorted by

Mr Moon. Driving through the wet and sleepy streets of Brumble Head the two men were silent, made thoughtful by the emptiness of the town. It lay like a cardboard replica beneath the mist and lamp-light and seemed hardly real. All that could be heard was the distant murmur of the sea, and the sound of voices floating from radios and television sets.

Although the streets were deserted Sergeant Watts obediently stopped at a red traffic light opposite Brumble railway bridge. A goods-train was coming slowly towards the hump-backed bridge, and as they watched a queer figure appeared crawling along the parapet. It was silhouetted by the smoke, and as the train passed beneath the bridge the figure jumped and disappeared.

The two men rushed from the car and up on to the bridge, but by the time they got there the train had passed, and nothing was to be seen on the tracks below them. They searched among the bushes beside the tracks, but still nothing was found. No doubt whatever they had seen had landed in one of the open carts of the goods-train.

Mr Moon suggested that as it was obviously pointless running after the train the matter ought to be handed over to Inspector Rice in nearby Llandridnod Wells, towards whose constabulary the train was heading. Sergeant Watts agreed, and returning to the foot of the bridge, he radioed in his report.

Mr Moon stayed on the bridge longer than his friend. Declining a lift home he gazed down at the wet tracks that led with such positive determination out of Brumble Head and into the world beyond. He thought of the courage that small figure must have possessed as it jumped down into the moving train, and thought how much he would have liked, long ago, to do something similar. To jump from a bridge and let fate as much as a train take him where it would. From his pocket he took the sealed note the doctor had given him

earlier. He crumpled it up and flung it away. 'I've no use for it,' he thought. He stood on the bridge in the mist and cold and smelt the tar and soaking brambles that filled the night. And then quite suddenly he decided to follow the figure to wherever it was going and, having nothing else to do with his life, to go there himself.

3

THE next morning Mr Moon wrote a few letters, paid off his outstanding bills, packed a small suitcase and then without bothering to lock his front door, got into his motor car and headed for Llandridnod Wells. It was a pleasant day for once, and the drive was uninterrupted until several miles from his destination he saw a hillside swarming with policemen. With them they had dogs, and people from the local village. He pulled into a layby where several police cars were parked and immediately sought out and was recognized by Inspector Rice who, before retirement had cast Moon into the drudgery of inactivity, had been his subordinate.

'Can't keep off the job, then?' asked the Inspector.

'Curiosity,' said Mr Moon, 'idle curiosity. It would seem you've not found the child yet. Any leads?'

'We searched the train when it came in last night,' said the Inspector, 'but we found nothing. He must have jumped off before it reached the station. Probably around here.' The Inspector waved his hand in the general direction of the surrounding hills.

'Have you any idea where he's heading?'

'None,' said the Inspector. 'All we've had is a false alarm. A farmer saw what he thought was a boy up on Bishops Hill, but it was hardly light and he could have been mistaken. His description was odd, he said the child was more like a dwarf.'

'Maybe it was.'

'Was what?'

'A dwarf.'

Inspector Rice insisted that such a notion was ridiculous.

'Then maybe it was a leprechaun,' said Mr Moon. 'It's not impossible.'

Inspector Rice didn't think the joke was funny. How Mr Moon could have been allowed to join the police force, let alone rise through the ranks, was a mystery to him. The man was full of preposterous theories, ranging from the view that the lost world of Atlantis would one day be discovered beneath the North Sea to a conviction that the belief in dragons was descended from prehistoric men, who had confused them with dinosaurs.

Later that day in a village pub a junior reporter asked Inspector Rice what everyone was looking for. Inspector Rice, who was cold, frustrated and tired, said: 'A leprechaun, you idiot.' The young reporter, an imaginative sort of chap, saw the possibilities in the story immediately. Into his mind's eye, clear and in large typeface, leapt the legendary headline POLICE SEEK LOST LEPRECHAUN! complete with exclamation mark.

'Well,' said the editor of the *Llandridnod and District News*, 'see if you can find out a bit more about this leprechaun. See if you can get a statement from the farmer who says he saw it.'

The reporter set out to find the farmer, who lived some miles away on the banks of the River Ludd.

'Of course it weren't a leprechaun,' said the farmer, locking the gate behind several cows. 'Of course it weren't. I never says it were.'

'But if leprechauns existed it might have been one, mightn't it?' asked the reporter.

'*If* they existed, yes,' answered the farmer.

*

The next day in the *Llandridnod and District News* appeared the strange story of how a farmer had seen a leprechaun on Bishops Hill, a well-known prehistoric spot. The leprechaun had been running at a tremendous speed and had seemed frightened. 'It is well known locally that Bishops Hill was once believed to be sacred, and that strange rites were performed upon its bleak slopes,' ran the article, 'and therefore the farmer's story might have a basis of truth.' The article went on less enthusiastically to say that Inspector Rice discounted the story about the leprechaun as a 'load of juvenile nonsense'. However, children in the neighbourhood did not share his views. Word of the leprechaun spread, and the rumour was well kindled, for soon a television crew in search of a light-hearted story was on its way through Much Wenlock to Llandridnod, via Presteigne and the River Ludd.

Casually on the 6 p.m. news, as a break from the various international disasters of the day, a television reporter asked Johnny Plackham, from Micawber Street, Steelborough, who was convalescing in Ludd from an excess of school, what he thought about the leprechaun rumoured to have been seen in the district. Johnny's immediate reply struck a chord in the hearts of the several thousand children watching.

Johnny said: 'I'd hide it from the likes of you and help it escape, that's what I'd do. You should let it alone.'

The next morning the newspapers thought this comment so marvellously funny that they ran a condescending article about the leprechaun and printed a picture of Johnny, with his words blazoned across their columns in large capital letters. The article was seen by thousands more children, some of whom took their scissors to it immediately.

Half an hour later in playgrounds all over Great Britain hordes of children were talking about and swearing allegiance to the leprechaun, wondering what it was doing, where it was heading, and how best they could help it. That evening it was discussed by them at 5.25 p.m. on BBC's 'Children's Panel' and 6.10 p.m. with Johnny Plackham on WTV's programme, 'Junior Talk-In'. They deplored the attitude of their elders and the audacity of the police in hunting the leprechaun as if it were a wild animal.

The first branch of the Secret Society for the Protection of Leprechauns was started by Johnny Plackham as soon as he returned home to Steelborough. He was excited by his sudden fame, and felt he had a special claim over the leprechaun. Within a week he had received six hundred letters from various parts of Britain, and had started one fund to raise money for the leprechaun and another to pay for stamps in order that the letters he'd received might be replied to. He became both President and Secretary of the Society and allowed everybody to start up their own branch of SSFTPOL for a small fee. Several of the letters were from Belgium and Holland, and one was from Cincinnati, sent by a boy who collected the names of submarines. Within a week SSFTPOL, or SPLOT, as it mysteriously became known, had spread to every major town and city in the land.

Johnny Plackham realized he was on to a good thing. He was cunning and sly and not the person he made himself out to be. He was far more interested in what he could make out of the leprechaun story than in the creature itself, which he didn't wholly believe existed anyway.

But Mr Moon's curiosity was gaining momentum. He joined in the search with much enthusiasm, not in the least discouraged by the fact that nothing was found. His zeal put the entire police force to shame and, much to Inspector Rice's annoyance, his officers would arrive at some distant spot only to discover that the place had already been searched thoroughly by Mr Moon. He was delighted to be active again, and was steadily becoming obsessed with whatever it was he was hunting. Be it child, leprechaun or dwarf, Mr Moon did not care.

His curiosity was to carry him to the brink of fairy-land itself.

4

THE dwarf found the anchor while working at the edge of the forest, clearing decayed trunks and branches that had fallen during the previous evening's storm. At first he thought it was a branch but when he could not lift it he scraped away moss and creepers and discovered it was made of iron. He called across the clearing to a friend working nearby to tell him of his discovery. Neither dwarf had seen an anchor before. Like maps they belonged to a bygone age, to a time when the world was reputed to have been different.

The village in which the dwarfs lived was called Oakwood, and the forest in which they worked ringed the village completely, leaving it in the utmost isolation. They believed the forest stretched on for ever, without end, broken only by a few clearings which sheltered villages similar to their own. The dwarfs possessed little curiosity and they saw no sense in venturing deeper into the forest than was thought necessary to gather the various kinds of mushroom that grew there. Once there had been pathways through the forest, but they had been allowed to fall into ruin and disappear centuries ago.

'It's an anchor, I'm sure it is.' The first dwarf ripped away the remaining creepers exposing barnacles and fossilized snails. 'Surely you've seen pictures of anchors? They're common enough.'

The idea that the anchor could be real was absurd to the

more logical of the dwarfs. The existence of anchors meant the existence of boats, and as far as he was concerned boats did not exist and oceans belonged to the world of fairy-tales.

'Somebody is playing a practical joke on us,' he said.

The dwarf who'd spoken first knew there was little point in trying to convince his friend that the anchor was real, but still he tried. 'This area of the forest is supposed to be enchanted,' he said. 'It is supposed to contain magic gates and other relics from the past.'

'Fiddle,' said his friend. 'Fiddle and bumph!'

The gates of which the first dwarf spoke were part and parcel of both their childhoods and figured in nearly every fairy-tale either of them had read. Any time two trees of equal dimensions were found together they were called Gates. They were supposed to be twins, to harbour strange powers and to grow simultaneously in two worlds. It was said that through these Gates humans could come to visit the real world and goblins and dwarfs could pass through into the human world.

'It's not fiddle,' said the first dwarf. 'You know the story of Greenweed, don't you? He didn't think it was fiddle and bumph. He was the dwarf who discovered some of the trees were magic. Remember how he built a boat out of one of them and sailed through into the human world? Marvellous story! Remember how on one of his journeys his boat drifted away and he was stranded for thirty years before finding similar Gates there?'

'Fiddle! Of course I know the story, but why did he bother building a boat? He could just have walked between the two trees and that would have worked well enough.'

The argument was one that was repeated over and over again, and while it never ended in a fight the dwarfs inevitably stomped off in opposite directions, both convinced that the other was stupid.

The dwarf who had found the anchor was called Nameon. Later in the day he returned alone to the place where he had been working. In the clearing small squat dragons sat chewing grass and wriggling uncomfortably in their harnesses. Their ancestors had been fierce creatures, spitting acid that burned like a flame; but goblins, gremlins, dwarfs and the rest, had tamed and bred them. Now they were used for hauling logs and for their thick green skins that, when stretched, made perfect coats and vests. In the winter they also provided food.

Nameon was a rarity among his kind. He possessed the matter-of-factness of most dwarfs, but he was a dreamer. He took only a passing interest in the everyday world, and when that interest had passed he returned to his dreams. He was sure the anchor was not a practical joke. It would have taken four or five dwarfs to carry it into the forest. What's more, one of its points was firmly buried in the roots of a tree. Or rather the roots had grown into the anchor.

Attached to one end of it was a chain. This too was coated in barnacles and rust. When he tugged at it the chain came clear of the earth, bringing up pebbles and worms. Some links were buried too deeply for him to pull clear and he had to dig the chain out with a knife. The chain snaked into the forest deeper than Nameon had been before, and the effort of uprooting and following it was beginning to exhaust him. He was on the brink of turning back when in front of him, standing perfectly upright among the trees, he saw a boat.

In its side was a gaping hole, and through it gurgled a stream no more than a foot across. The remnant of what had once been a wide river, its banks were buried beneath a century of fallen leaves and flowers. Several feet from the bow of the ship the remains of a figurehead protruded from the earth. Its nose and lips had been worn away, and one cheek and the whole of a shoulder had been scarred by a woodpecker. It lolled to one side and, buried waist-deep as it was, it was still noticeably taller than the dwarf.

Inside, the floor of the boat had rotted into the ground which was thick with bluebells. On a cabin table now supported by strands of creeper and a single leg was a tin box split open by rain. In it Nameon found what appeared to be bronze necklaces and rings. Tucked away in a separate compartment was a piece of pigskin. He took it from the box and unfolded it. To his astonishment he found it was an ancient and perfectly preserved map. Though the back was covered in mould the picture was still visible. It was nine inches square, and in the top right-hand corner was written 'Greenweed's map'. Along the bottom, in smaller writing, it said: 'The ways back from the human world are hard to find. The one known route lies in the north of that world between twin oaks that stand at a peninsula's end where pine forest and waters meet.'

Nameon carefully refolded the map and explored further. On the ground under the mossy frame of a bunk was a huge book. Its cover was bound in pigskin and scrawled on it were the words, 'Greenweed's Journal, His Adventures and Wanderings in Humanland'. But the pages inside had been made of ordinary paper, and its contents had provided a banquet for termites and ants.

The dwarf felt bewildered standing in the broken and gloomy shell, but the sensation was not unpleasant and he wanted it to last. With the knife he had used to unearth the chain he carved his name into the side of a lifeboat that had crashed down through the rotting deck and into the cabin. Thus, dwarf-fashion, he marked and laid claim to the boat. It was hard work. The scent of bluebells and wood anemones thickened the already clammy atmosphere, making him drowsy. The dwarf sat on the edge of the lifeboat, looking up through the broken deck into the mass of leaves and branches

above him. Through them he could make out patches of sky, no longer blue but pink. 'It must be late,' he yawned. He felt uncomfortable on the edge of the lifeboat. He climbed into it, and curling up into a ball Nameon fell asleep.

5

Somewhere on the outskirts of Llandridnod Wells at precisely 2.29 in the morning a small figure clad in a rain-cloak jumped from the open cart of a goods-train and scrambled off across the soaking fields.

Nameon did not know why he was running or exactly what he was running away from, but instinct told him to keep on the move until some form of shelter could be found. He was frightened, disorientated and confused. It was panic that had made him leap on to the goods-train, and now that his panic had subsided he was concerned solely with safety; the terror he had felt on waking he forced to the back of his mind. He did not even try to guess why he had not woken in his own world and in the same boat. A power such as that contained within the twin trees was unpredictable, and his dilemma was serious enough without idle speculation.

Little could be distinguished through the darkness and drizzle. The few people he had seen so far had been twice his size, the buildings had smelt overpoweringly of salt and the only magical thing that had happened was that he'd not been caught.

He did not run through the open fields, but kept to the hedgerows till he found a gap large enough to crawl through. On the far side of the hedge was a steep lane and Nameon decided to follow it, moving uphill and away from the railway track. He trudged for several slow miles before the hedgerows on either side fell away to reveal a complex of barnyards. Stopping to shelter was out of the question, for on examining the barns he discovered they were occupied by large moon-eyed creatures that groaned solemnly and wore round their necks enormous bells. It was hours later when he finally found a place he considered safe.

The cottage was tiny and dilapidated. It was hidden by a line of trees and Nameon discovered it simply because he preferred walking among the trees rather than along the lane, which mud had made almost impassable. Behind the trees was moorland and the cottage roof had been outlined against a flat horizon. There were no pathways leading to the cottage so he trampled through the wet bracken, bending it and leaving a wake behind as if some impossible yacht had sailed there. It was false dawn when he reached the cottage and after surveying the surrounding land he crept stealthily inside.

The cottage consisted of two small rooms, the smallest of which was completely empty but for a sink blocked with leaves and a rusty bucket in which lay a frog, either hibernating or frozen to death. The other room contained cupboards, a fire-grate and a large old-fashioned armchair. The place smelled of neglect and decay.

It was winter and there was little activity in the country-side. At night the wind was sharp and loud and it was not the best of times to be sleeping rough. But the dwarf slept in the armchair without discomfort, and was eventually woken by the sound of rain crashing on to corrugated iron someone had used to patch the roof.

Nameon decided to light a fire. He gathered bits of paper and burnable objects from among the rubble, which he first poked with a stick to make sure nothing dangerous was living beneath it. From his cloak he took burning flint and wick, and struck one till the other caught alight. Biting off a piece of the wick he set it among the damp wood and paper. But at best the fire smouldered, adding no warmth to the place. He set the cottage in order, and spent part of the afternoon examining pictures found in stacks of damp newspapers. In this way he gleaned bits of information. He learned that the world he had just entered regarded as normal many of the things he had previously considered magical, and thus the whole fabric of the fairy-tales he had been taught as a child began to crumble.

Tales of the human world had been passed on by old dwarfs who had known Greenweed personally (or so they had said) and later by their children, and in passing down the years they had become in parts forgotten, in parts exaggerated. It seemed there were no Dodo birds, no fabulous beasts. Among the hundreds of pictures he examined he saw neither a winged horse nor a unicorn. Still, because he could not distinguish between advertisements and realistic photographs he gained a false impression of abundance and colour, one completely at odds with what he had seen so far. But Nameon was intelligent and though for a while this seeming abundance puzzled him he eventually decided that even in the human world fact and fantasy were hopelessly mixed, and that what was real and unreal would in time sort itself out. Pictures of motor cars intrigued him, as did pictures of cities, but the latter he dismissed as morbid fantasies, possibly due to the fact that the pictures were of slums in places such as Glasgow and Calcutta.

His most important discovery was that there existed human beings nearly as small as himself. They were certainly not children, for children he could easily recognize by the clearness of their skin and lack of years carved into their faces. He saw no reason why there should not be some humans as small as himself, considering the reverse sometimes happened in Oakwood. One dwarf in living memory was reputed to have grown to a height of nearly five feet. Nameon realized that if he was disguised he could move about with some degree of freedom in his new world and he made his plans accordingly.

Late in the afternoon when the fire finally caught, he went out to gather wood. It was sparse, but he wanted to make a pile and keep the fire burning during the night. On one of his expeditions, just as the light was failing, he noticed in the distance a small village, its outline camouflaged by the colour of the moor. From a distance it looked small enough to run from quickly if anything went amiss, and so he decided to investigate. In the cottage over his own clothes he put bits and pieces which he'd found lying in cupboards, and over these wrapped his rain-cloak. His problem about height was eased, if not solved, by a huge pair of boots he found hidden under the chair. They were uncomfortable, but by stuffing folded newspapers into them he made himself nearly seven inches taller. He pulled loose planks across the doorway in a feeble attempt to keep the warmth in, and then hobbled off in the direction of the village.

Nameon had dreamt so often of what he would do when faced with peculiar events, that more than any realist he felt able to cope with his situation. As he crossed the moor he tried to read the constellations above him, but he recognized only a few. His two favourite signs, the Oak-leaf and the Dog-rose were visible, but the rest were lost in a swarm the size and brilliance of which stunned him. There were more stars than even he had ever imagined. They were like a mass of phosphorescent daisies on a dark and endless lawn.

Nightly in his own world he had joined in futile conversations about the stars. Some dwarfs maintained there were only those that could be seen from the village green, and they had actually counted them. There were, according to these dwarfs, one thousand nine hundred and forty-six all told, while other dwarfs, including Nameon, said the stars, like the forest, went on forever.

The village and the moorland met abruptly at a grey stone wall. On one side was wilderness and on the other stone houses. At first glance the differences between Nameon's village and the one in front of him were superficial. The dwellings were angular rather than rounded, the pathways well laid and straight rather than circular. It seemed incredible that but for the low wall there was nothing to protect the village or its inhabitants from attack.

There was one main street in the village and in the middle of the street, lit by a fluctuating lightbulb, was a sign that read 'The Drowned Duck'. The prospect of food and drink helped him overcome his natural fear of the village. He crept down the street for a closer look at the building. Its windows were set low into the stones, and with a little effort Nameon could see inside. But for one man standing behind a wooden counter, the place was empty. To Nameon's delight on the counter was a tray of pies, and behind it rows of mugs and bottles, which suggested the place was not unlike a mead hall. It differed rather drastically from the mead halls in his own world, however, being much smaller and having about it the atmosphere of a private room, rather than of a stable. He could see no barrels anywhere, but this did not deter him and taking his life in his hands Nameon hobbled inside. The folded-up newspapers in his boots gave him some confidence, but he was still tiny by human standards. Although he seemed embarrassed by Nameon's unorthodox appearance the landlord mistook him for a human being immediately. He attempted to be cordial and asked: 'What's yours?'

Nameon's relief must have been visible. Although the landlord's words sounded clumsy and without poetry it was possible for the dwarf to understand them.

'I'll have a sweet mead,' he said, 'and lots of those.' He pointed hungrily to a tray of pies on the counter. His stomach rumbled and his mouth watered.

'Sweet *what?*' asked the landlord, puzzled as much by the stranger's accent as request.

'Sweet mead.'

The landlord frowned. 'We don't have it here,' he said.

The meetings of great men and the turning points in history are never quite as impressive in reality as they are in the imagination, and thus this historic meeting between two worlds went unnoticed by Mr Thomas Butler, the landlord of the Drowned Duck. He rummaged under the bar-counter muttering to himself about foreigners, and when he re-surfaced presented Nameon with a bottle of brown ale, poured into a glass that was difficult to handle. Still frowning, he disappeared into a room behind the bar, leaving Nameon to struggle with the huge glass.

6

'A DWARF's just come into the bar, Gweneth.'

'A what?'

'A dwarf.'

'Don't be daft, Thomas.'

'He's extraordinary, Gweneth, take a look for yourself. He's odd as a left boot.'

Gweneth Butler put down her knitting and waddled through the tiny living-room towards the bar. She was a vast lady, twice the girth of her husband and treble his weight. She commanded the Drowned Duck as a business tycoon might command his empire, and she had about her the same strictness and eye for detail as a school-teacher. She was a warm but fussy creature. The wooden pumps at the bar were highly polished and the flower-print cushions on the hard-backed chairs were always clean, the curtains were neatly arranged and the plastic flowers on the window ledges dusted daily. Hers was one of the three public houses that served the village's population of one hundred and ninety-nine, a figure that for some unaccountable reason never fluctuated. If anyone were to seek out the parish registers and examine them, they would discover that for over three centuries the village of Penmoor had neither grown nor shrunk. People had died and others had been born, but it was done neatly and with an astonishing regularity and regard for balance.

Though competition between the public houses was

tough, with the locals the Drowned Duck was the most popular, especially since Mrs Butler had installed a television set. Her clientele, if not quite as well-mannered and besuited as those that graced the Eaton and the Prince of Wales, were jollier to serve. They were mostly farm folk and as the main product of Penmoor was sheep, they were mostly sheep-farmers. Of the Eaton's clientele only a few were locals, the rest being young men who arrived in bright red sports cars from Llandridnod Wells, thirteen miles away across the moor.

Mrs Butler peeped through the beaded curtains at the back of the bar and saw at a corner table the cause of her husband's consternation. The small gentleman (she considered all her customers, no matter how odd, as gentlemen) was watching the television set with such concentration that she suspected he had not seen one before. He was fascinated: his huge knotted hands, so out of proportion to the rest of him, clutched the arms of the chair, and he seemed to have stopped breathing. The landlady glowed with pride, for televisions were still a rarity in Penmoor, and his rapt attention confirmed her belief that the set had indeed been a good investment. Soon, she thought, after the main news was over and as the weekly serial began, her customers would start tumbling in. The first to come would be Mr Badger, old and grumbling, who lived next door but three. And then perhaps Mrs Hayes and her husband William might appear for their two crisps and a stout. But for the moment at least the bar was empty. Mrs Butler pushed her bulk through the beaded curtains (a rather exotic present from her younger sister who had once visited Spain) and, trailing a clean white cloth across the counter, she addressed the peculiar little gentleman.

'You're a stranger, then?'

Nameon jumped, almost upsetting his glass. He had been

so engrossed in the marvellous images that he'd forgotten where he was. The booming voice of Gweneth Butler reminded him. She was as large as any lady giant the illustrators of the story-stones* had imagined. Three of Oakwood's burliest goblins combined would have hardly been a match for her. She wore a long blue smock dotted with marigolds, her face was painted and her hair piled up on her massive head. She was indeed a product of every dwarf's childhood, she was what one stopped believing in once one had grown up.

The first humans had made no deep impression on Nameon. Except for Mr Butler they had been figures in the distance, and even Mr Butler himself had made no real impression, for he was a shrivelled, pinch-faced little man. Though the woman in front of him was huge, she looked friendly and he recognized her warmth immediately. Perhaps if someone else had appeared in front of him and broken his concentration he would have trembled and run from the place. But women such as Mrs Butler, in the story-stones at least, were more preoccupied with love than with violence.

'Yes, I am a stranger,' he said, answering her question. And then he was lost for something else to say.

Mrs Butler took his silence for embarrassment. Surely, she thought, such little people cannot feel quite at home anywhere, and are constantly and slyly scrutinized, and threatened by all objects larger than themselves.

'Well then,' she said. 'Well then.' She sat down beside him, her vastness overflowing and all but hiding the chair, till she

---

*Story-stones: since pigskin was expensive, fairy-tales and other literature were often painted on to flat stones which were propped up against a wall to be read. Story-stones were popular for they could not be ripped or chewed by young dwarfs, and distribution caused no problem as they were made and painted within the village.

seemed suspended in air between the table and the pale green linoleum. 'Well then!' Her exclamations reverberated around his glass, and he waited apprehensively for the woman to interrogate him.

Mrs Butler's manners would never allow her to poke into Nameon's business and ask what he was doing in Penmoor, but she did allow herself the luxury of asking where he had come from. When Nameon answered awkwardly 'Oakwood', she admitted she had never heard of the place, and that it was obviously a long way off. Nameon agreed. It was foreign, he said, and probably a long way away, though he wasn't quite sure how far.

'It accounts for the way you speak,' she said, and only just stopped herself from adding, 'It accounts for the way you look.'

She could not help feeling that her guest was more than just foreign. In her book foreigners were people who were either very dark or very blond or extremely yellow. She fancied that during her life she must have seen, either in person or in the more exotic cases in photographs, at least one member of all the races that inhabit the earth. All races, that is, except for the one to which her present customer belonged. She could no more place him than she could have placed a visitor from outer space. But for the gigantic boots which she recognized as hobnails and the cloak which she mistook for a cyclist's cape, most of his clothes were unidentifiable. His features were more weatherbeaten than even the roughest farmer's, and this suggested to Mrs Butler that he had come from a northern country, probably from one of those dark, brooding places in which many a fairy-tale was set. His hands were coarse, like gloves that had been left to dry in front of a fire and then forgotten. His nose was broken, his skin was pitted, his ears were thick, yet his teeth were perfectly white. But more than these features it was his eyes that puzzled her. They were like the eyes of a child gazing out from behind an ancient mask; eyes not dulled in the slightest by over-familiarity with objects or time.

After a few polite words, none of which made any sense to Nameon, Mrs Butler rose from her chair and returned to the bar, satisfied that her customer, though unusual, was pleasant enough.

Behind the bar her husband Thomas stood holding an unfamiliar coin. 'He paid with this,' he said. It was a wafer-thin coin, one that in Nameon's world could purchase mead, bread, smoking leaves, goats' milk and other necessities.

'It looks rare,' said Gweneth.

'Aye, it is,' said Thomas, eyeing Nameon to check that he was not listening.

'It's the rarest coin I've seen.' He fiddled with the coin, turning it in his fingers to see if there was something written on it that he had missed.

'It could be from a fun-fair,' implied Mrs Butler. 'You know, the things you put in machines.'

On one side of the coin was an acorn, and on the other a hollyhock. It was a dull gold colour and looked impressive.

'This isn't from a fun-fair,' said Thomas. 'It's foreign.'

Thomas, an obsessive coin collector whose life was spent in the hope of finding treasures, clutched the coin tightly. 'We'll accept it and have it valued when we go into town,' he said. Mrs Butler nodded her approval, believing utterly in her husband's instinct for such things as rare finds. She agreed that a foreigner so obviously foreign, who possibly had no other money and no way of getting hold of any, should be allowed to pay in gold coins if he wished.

Nameon had now been in the Drowned Duck for half an hour, and during this time had hardly taken his eyes from the television, for he was convinced it was a crystal ball of the most superb quality.

He found what it told him about the world rather unnerving. It seemed no communities were protected by oak forests, and so quite naturally many communities were at war with one another, causing much confusion and unnecessary pain. Everywhere, if the crystal was to be believed, were groups of humans whose job it was to kill each other, and evil magicians who had the power to poison the earth and turn the rain into acid. On the moors he had seen no evidence of such stupidity, and so after a time he grew dubious as to the crystal's accuracy. It seemed to jump at random between the past, the present and the future, and so far it had not touched upon the personal details of his life. He knew it would, if he waited long enough, and so he was determined to watch it for days if necessary.

The first of the regular customers to arrive in the pub was Mr Pike, who was unusually old and who did nothing. He shuffled across the room and did not notice Nameon till he tried to sit down in the seat Nameon already occupied. He did not bother to say 'excuse me' but grunting he stood up and moved to the next available table. Mr Pike was a little blind, though some said it was his mind rather than his eyes that was blind, for he'd stopped bothering with all but the essentials of the world. His whiskey was one essential, another was his bed, and a third was the smell of moorland that drifted daily through his nostrils and across his tongue.

While Mrs Butler was setting the whiskey down in front of Mr Pike, Nameon slid from his chair and strode purposefully towards the door. He said, 'Till the leaves reopen,'* as matter-of-factly as he could, then hurried outside. It was one thing to sit comfortably drinking mead and crystal-gazing,

---

* In Nameon's world the nights are colder than in our world and on many trees the leaves curl up against the cold, opening at dawn like flowers. The expression simply means, 'until tomorrow'.

but quite another to be sat upon by an absent-minded giant.

Mrs Butler stared after him, about to ask what he meant, when Mr Pike accidentally spilt his whiskey while reaching across the table for an imaginary pot of jam, quite similar to the jam he had eaten at home only a few minutes ago. 'Where's the butter?' he asked, eclipsing even Nameon's peculiar remark.

Outside Nameon felt unsteady. The stark street shook his confidence and nothing seemed matter-of-fact at all. The grey houses had about them a clarity that menaced him; it was as if they, unlike those who had built them, knew what he was and could whisper his secret whenever they chose.

On his way back to the cottage Nameon dwelt on the first sentence Mrs Butler had uttered. 'You're a stranger, then?' she had asked, and it had seemed more a statement than a question. Indeed he was a stranger, more so than he had felt able to explain. He imagined Greenweed centuries ago, arriving one evening in his boat at the mouth of an estuary wider than all his own world seemed. He imagined the wind, and the squawk of sea birds as that first stranger stepped from his ill-fated craft and crossed the unpopulated marshlands in search of – of what? Of a way back home surely. For what else would someone who is lost search for?

He trudged along, and the thoughts that dominated his mind were of home. He fingered the pigskin map in his pocket, but it gave him little comfort. It was old and by now the years might easily have obliterated the way back. He was a stranger in the deepest sense of all; he was not among his own kind.

7

WHILST Inspector Rice was still under the misapprehension that the object of their search was a runaway child, Mr Moon's fancies were moving in a more positive direction. The idea that the child was really a dwarf, which he had jokingly suggested earlier, seemed not such a bad idea after all. The fact that he had no real evidence was not something to deter Mr Moon. He spent several mornings in the local library delving among books on fairies and magic, and the more he read the more plausible his idea seemed. From what he could deduce it was only at the turn of the century that stories about goblins and leprechauns visiting men tailed off. He guessed that since that time the world had become too crowded, or that some natural disaster had befallen them.

Once Mr Moon had an idea he was unable to stop it growing. Eventually it occupied all his waking moments and swamped his dreams, and it was for this reason more than any other that he was considered eccentric by those who knew him. His ideas did not run in straight lines (what Inspector Rice would call 'lateral thinking') but moved crabwise, picking up on their journey all manner of fanciful notions.

So far no one had claimed 'the child', and the Missing Persons Bureau had had no notification of any being lost. For Mr Moon this was almost enough to balance the odds in favour of the child being a dwarf. Why an anonymous child should be on the run was a mystery the police had been unable to solve. No crimes had been committed locally that could be linked to a small person, and the Brumble Head and District Harbour Board showed no interest whatsoever in the matter. Thus when Mr Moon suggested to Inspector Rice that it was rather a trivial affair and hardly worth the attention of the entire Llandridnod Wells Constabulary, Inspector Rice agreed and the hunt was called off, leaving Mr Moon the only person still interested in the matter. The few journalists who had remained hanging about closed their notebooks and went home, as did the local busybodies. Only one television crew remained at the scene. Having brought their cameras a great distance they wanted to keep the story alive and were dismayed by the police action. They decided to visit Inspector Rice in Llandridnod Wells Police Station and complain.

'Surely there must be a new angle we can latch on to?' asked the chief cameraman, who hated not getting his own way.

'I'm sure there is,' said Inspector Rice. And he told them how Mr Moon had been spending his time in the library reading books about goblins.

'He's starting to think there are leprechauns running about Wales. He has of course retired from the police force,' he said by way of explanation. The camera crew nodded solemnly. They thanked Inspector Rice for his information and set off to find Mr Moon.

It was the boredom of routine that was responsible for Mr Moon's urge to go running about the countryside in search of dwarfs. Routine had been ingrained deeply into the fabric of his life. From sunrise to sunset he had lived a life of routine, his world was one in which nothing was ever out of place and in which all unusual and unexpected things were soon strangled. As with all routines, he had finally grown bored.

Mr Moon had grown bored long before he had had the chance to grow old. But to rebel against routine is one of the most difficult rebellions, and until now Mr Moon had never had an alternative. But now the alternative was clear to him. It was to hunt for something beyond his normal reach and leave all else behind.

He reasoned that if he appeared to be insane nobody would take him seriously, and therefore no one else would bother hunting the creature. So when he was interviewed on television, Mr Moon chose to answer the questions put to him with an innocence it is presumed only the mad possess.

Nameon saw the interview while sitting alone in the bar of the Drowned Duck the following evening. Mrs Butler, stationed behind the bar and cleaning already perfectly clean brandy glasses, did not. Nor did Thomas, who was in one of the upstairs rooms gloating over a new addition to his coin collection.

The face of the interviewer appeared in the crystal. It was a spotty face, and its thin practised smiled annoyed Nameon. He would have turned away from the screen had not the countryside looked almost familiar.

The interviewer began, 'This afternoon the local police called off a search that has been fascinating this small district of Wales for several days.

'Following reports that a child was seen leaping on to a goods-train from a bridge in Brumble Head, police with tracker dogs have been combing the surrounding hills. So far no evidence has been found of a runaway child, and now rumour has it that it might not be a child at all but – hard as it is to believe in this day and age – a leprechaun!'

Nameon stirred uneasily in his chair and glanced towards Mrs Butler. She was now polishing a liqueur bottle that had stood behind the counter unopened for eleven years, and she was oblivious to all else.

The face in the crystal continued: 'Although the hunt has now been officially abandoned there are those who insist there has been no false alarm. Indeed, there are those who insist the leprechaun theory to be valid, and one such person is nothing less than a retired police officer, Mr Reginald Moon.'

From the crystal came the sound of dramatic music and the camera drew back to reveal Mr Moon standing uncomfortably against a backdrop of Welsh mountains. He was dressed in baggy grey trousers and a brown tweed coat. Out of one pocket hung a red handkerchief and from the other peeped a well-thumbed mystery novel. The interviewer now wore a serious expression, and in his hand held what looked like an iron lollipop attached to a long piece of flex. He thrust this object into Mr Moon's face.

'Are you serious about continuing this search alone?' he asked. Mr Moon smiled benignly at the pimply youth and said, 'Yes, I am quite serious.'

'But why, when the whole of Llandridnod Wells police force have abandoned the hunt? Do you really think there is a child lost in the hills?'

'Child? Who said anything about a child?' Mr Moon's expression was one of complete surprise. 'I never said anything about a child being lost.'

'You mean you don't think it's a child?' asked the interviewer, encouraging him.

'Of course I don't. What else could it be but a leprechaun? I know about leprechauns. They are taking over the world. Hordes of them. They are creeping out from rabbit-holes and infiltrating the country.'

The interviewer successfully stifled a smile. 'We know children have formed some sort of society to protect the

35

creature,' he said, 'but don't you think that coming from a man of your age and position the whole idea is, well, perhaps a little ridiculous?'

Mr Moon did not seem to mind that the question was insulting. He blinked and affirmed, 'Certainly not, my age and position have nothing to do with the matter. Anyway, nothing is more ridiculous than anything else.'

'Can you describe this creature?' asked the interviewer.

'No,' said Mr Moon, 'I haven't seen it clearly yet. But if you wish me to hazard a guess I'd say it was about two-and-a-half feet tall.'

Mr Moon answered the questions in such a serious manner that people watching began to feel sorry for him. The interviewer himself began to regret teasing the man and was about to bring the interview to a close when Mr Moon rushed up to the camera and, taking off his hat, whispered, 'Avoid rabbit-holes!' The astonished cameraman held the shot long enough for all those watching to decide that Mr Moon was silly and that the leprechaun was a figment of his disordered imagination, which is exactly what Mr Moon wanted them to believe.

He had made his point. From that moment on no adult entertained the notion that a leprechaun might possibly exist. By the simple trick of appearing insane he had returned the concept of goblins, leprechauns and other such beings back to the realm of childhood. The screen faded to some other, more terrible news.

It did not matter to Mr Moon if he seemed ridiculous, for the opinion of others no longer had any influence over his life. He longed to believe it was a mythical creature he was hunting. In his childhood he had been passionately convinced of their existence, and even when he had reached an age when such things ought to be disregarded he had stubbornly clung to his beliefs. Ridicule had not changed his

36

mind, and it had been with sorrow that he had noticed his companions grow stubborn and matter-of-fact about the world. Now he was old his beliefs were still intact, and he was determined not to let Inspector Rice or anyone else pull them apart. During the whole of his career he had worked diligently and had risen through the ranks despite his quirks of character. He had solved many mysteries, but few had fired his imagination. Here at last was one that did. A few clues and his lingering doubts as to the nature of the creature would be swept aside.

Nameon, sitting in the Drowned Duck, found the interview fascinating. He realized Mr Moon was not a malicious person, but also realized that neither was he insane. Why he pretended to be insane was obvious: he wished to discredit Nameon's existence, and the reason was also obvious: he wanted to hunt Nameon alone.

Unfortunately the crystal had not seen fit to forecast what would happen if the ex-detective caught up with Nameon. He doubted if Mr Moon would hold him captive, but he could not be certain, and his uncertainty was enough to put him on his guard and make him vow to avoid Mr Moon at all costs. He hurriedly drained his glass, stuffed a pie into his pocket and once again shouting, 'Till the leaves reopen,' he stepped out into the night.

'What does he mean, "till the leaves reopen"?' asked Mrs Butler. 'It's twice he's said that.'

'It's a foreign expression,' said her husband, 'very rare.' He jangled Nameon's strange coins in his pocket, hardly able to contain his greed.

8

A COLD wind blew drizzle in from the moors. The Drowned Duck's signboard creaked and complained. Other sounds were the distant baaing of sheep and the clatter of soup plates from behind tiny curtained windows. Behind a door not sixty yards away Mr Pike was wiping jam from his white silk scarf and putting on his overcoat, ready to venture out into the night. Across the road Mrs Hayes was telling her husband William that it was time for crisps and stout, and in a narrow hallway stuffed with two lifetimes of bric-à-brac a highly polished grandfather clock ticked and echoed within itself, summoning up the energy for a single chime.

It was 6.30 in the evening. For a moment Nameon sat on the thick granite steps of the public house gazing absently at his boots. Then he stood up and, pulling his cloak tightly around him, hurried off towards the cottage.

After the initial shock of Mr Moon's appearance in the crystal he was calmer and quite decisive about what action he must take. Tonight would be his last night in the cottage. He felt he was wasting time. Greenweed's map gave no indication as to how far away the Gates were, but he knew, however far, it would be farther than he had ventured in his life.

It was beginning to rain heavily. Pools appeared where the pavements and road had been damaged and where, earlier, village children had successfully dammed the drains with stones and bracken. At a tiny intersection to the High Street Nameon stopped to take a final look at the village, astonished as ever by the stillness of this unfamiliar world, in which everything seemed at peace and from which, contrary to the tales he had heard and the visions he had seen in the crystal, violence seemed absent.

His reverie was interrupted by a distant coughing and spluttering. For a moment the image flashed through his mind of the forests around Oakwood, and he imagined the sound to be that of wood-dragon, hoarsely coughing and yelping through a tangle of leaves and roots.

The road that fed into the high street was on a steep hill. It was cobbled, bleak, and glittering. On either side were squat houses with tiny sandstone window-sills and doorsteps worn down by a century of boots. The coughing grew louder, and up the hill crawled what looked like a huge beetle. Nameon sheltered under the canopy of a nearby confectionery shop. He squatted with his back against the tiled wall, and watched as the thing lumbered on without deviating from its chosen path. Miraculously, it had not seen him. At the top of the hill it spluttered, shuddered and stopped. Then something happened that gave Nameon a nasty jolt.

A part of the creature opened and from out of it stepped a human being wrapped from head to toe in oilskins. Nameon crept forward to the edge of the pavement, both repelled and fascinated by the spectacle. The man walked to the front of the creature and kicked it violently. He then forcibly opened its mouth and without so much as a moment's hesitation stuck his head inside it. Nameon crossed the road, which was as far as he dared go, and waited with apprehension for it to snap its jaws shut over the man's head. But it did nothing of the kind. The man withdrew his head of his own accord, and slamming the poor creature's mouth shut he climbed back inside.

*

It was the forceful slamming of the motor car's bonnet more than any technical skill on the part of the driver that seemed to do the trick. Once more the motor spluttered into life, and the car continued on up the hill.

When it passed him Nameon recognized it from pictures he had seen in magazines at the cottage and in the crystal, and he realized it was an artificial device, not an animal. He wondered if it minded not being alive, or if it even knew. Outside the Drowned Duck it stopped again and again the oilskin-clad figure stepped out of it. For a moment the man's face was lit by the single bulb that hung above the pub's signboard, and a moment was all Nameon needed to recognize it as the face of Mr Moon.

9

THE search for the dwarf had led Mr Moon to the tiny village of Penmoor.

He had spent a restless afternoon in Llandridnod Wells with Inspector Rice who after the television fiasco felt acutely embarrassed in his company. Mr Moon had sat on the floor studying an ordnance survey map of the district while up-and-coming young policemen manoeuvred round him carrying cups of tea. He muttered to himself, unable to concentrate for the persistent ringing of telephones, an inescapable feature of all police stations. He came to the conclusion that Bishops Hill would be the best starting-point for his search, and by midday he had departed, much to the relief of Inspector Rice who had seriously considered arresting him for loitering.

Bishops Hill was a couple of miles outside Llandridnod Wells. It was a depressingly ordinary and unmagical looking hill, and between it and the next town was nothing but moorland, with tiny Penmoor stuck in the centre, a distant outpost invaded for several weeks of the year by enthusiastic hikers before being once more forgotten. Instinct told Mr Moon to go there, instinct and the fact that there was nowhere else to go.

He drove slowly across the moor, his eyes constantly searching the horizon but seeing little except sheep and the monotonous bracken. As he drove the sky changed and the clouds piled up on one another until all distances were lost in mist. That day an elephant could have tiptoed across the moor unseen.

It was dark and beginning to rain heavily when he reached Penmoor. His car moved up the road, coughing and spluttering. The windscreen wipers hardly worked, and the headlamps distorted shadows, making everything look grotesque. At one point, just before his car broke down (his technical skill had put the fault right in a moment) he imagined he saw a dog or a small human figure crouched under the awning of a shopfront, but when he drew level with the shop he saw nothing. The street was empty, and the only public building that was lit was the Drowned Duck. He decided it would suit his needs perfectly, and inquired if there was a room available for the evening.

Mr Moon had had a life-long love of hotels. Not of grand hotels, which were anyway beyond his means, but of small and anonymous hotels that remained for ever without a sense of importance, as if importance would somehow lead to their ruin. He loved hotels that drew no attention to themselves, hotels that bordered on the invisible. People passed through them and left nothing behind. Character was swept from them like dust. Rumpled sheets were cleaned, ashtrays were emptied and new soap was placed neatly on the washbasin's brim. In such hotels the guests had no need to put on airs of grandeur, and strangers were thrown together whether they liked it or not. And this was fine by Mr Moon.

Such were his thoughts while Mrs Butler prepared his room above the bar of the Drowned Duck.

He sat drinking in the Snug, a tiny room behind the main bar. His oilskin coat had been hurriedly grabbed from him and hung in a passageway where it was allowed to drip to its heart's content in the company of several umbrellas. A few regular customers were settled in front of the television in the public bar and as it was unlikely that they would be ordering any more beer until the commercial break Mr Butler, who disliked television, joined Mr Moon in the Snug.

He was not a talkative man and did not offer to strike up a conversation. He sat engrossed in the current issue of *Coins and Coin Collectors*, his favourite magazine, and he searched its pages in vain for any coins that resembled those he had been given by Nameon. Disgruntled at discovering nothing, he wandered upstairs to the room in which he kept back copies of the magazine. Mr Moon was meanwhile absent-mindedly jingling coins in his pockets and listening to the sound of gunshots drifting in from the next room. Wondering how much loose change he possessed he took out his money and counted it.

Among the coins was one larger than the rest. On one side was an acorn and on the other a plough. He had watched Mr Butler studying his magazine and had been intrigued by the disappointed grunts that had issued from behind it. He realized that the landlord must have given him the coin in his change by mistake and so when Mr Butler, arms loaded with dusty magazines, returned, Mr Moon gave it back.

'It looks unusual,' he said.

'Aye,' said the landlord, 'too unusual.' He dumped the magazines down on the table. 'It's foreign you see, and they're the hardest to identify.'

He was making ready to thumb through the back issues when he was called to the bar. The guns had stopped and now a disembodied voice was praising the advantages of new washing-powder. The commercials were under way and people wanted their glasses filled.

In his hurry to get the serving of drinks over with the

44

landlord left the coin on top of the magazines and Mr Moon re-examined it.

Its oddness disturbed him. The coin was certainly not minted by any modern machinery, but neither did it look old. The engraving of the acorn was realistic enough, but the plough was unlike any plough he had seen. It looked medieval, and though the blade was large the shaft was smaller than normal, as if it had been fashioned for a child rather than for a grown man.

When the screeching of car tyres and the sound of gunshots resumed Mr Butler returned to the Snug. He settled his thin frame into a chair and was about to continue his search among the magazines when Mr Moon interrupted him.

'It's a nice coin,' he said, 'where did you find it?'

Mr Butler looked up, but did not answer. He felt uneasy. He had never quite convinced himself that taking the coins from the stranger did not constitute theft. He was so obsessed with his hobby that a windfall of this nature seemed a miracle, and he constantly expected the little man to reappear with a band of policemen and reclaim the coins. He had hidden them in various nooks and crannies about the pub and the coin now on the table was one he had been given less than an hour ago, and which he had absent-mindedly put in the till.

Seeing that his question disturbed the landlord, Mr Moon tried a subtler approach. 'I suppose you must receive many of your coins from customers?' he asked.

'I always make it worth their while,' said the landlord. 'After all one coin is no use to someone who doesn't collect them. They're of no real value unless part of a set.'

'True,' said Mr Moon, although he knew it was not true at all. 'Have you possessed that particular coin for long?'

'A foreigner . . .' began Mr Butler, but now a new wave of guilt swept over him and he did not finish the sentence. He wished his wife would come back from preparing the inquisitive stranger's room and help him out of his awkward conversation. But Mr Moon persisted.

'Can you describe the foreigner to me?'

Mr Butler fiddled with the magazines. 'The coin's not stolen, is it?' he asked. 'If it is, I want nothing to do with it.'

'Stolen?' said Mr Moon. 'Stolen? I really don't know. I'm a bit of a collector myself, and simply curious about it.'

With this Mr Butler once more felt at ease. 'Why,' he thought, 'the lodger's interest is purely academic.' Without hesitation he launched into a description of the original owner of the coin. So enthusiastic was he that he told of the other coins he had 'exchanged' and spoke at length about the odd clothes his benefactor had worn. He described the obviously padded hobnail boots, the oddly styled cloak and the craggy face. He even tried to imitate the way the stranger had spoken, and told of the previously unheard-of expression he had used. 'Every night he says the same thing, "Till the leaves reopen", he says, and then he's out like a shot. The wife thinks he's shy, but I reckon he's daft. He's certainly not from these parts.'

In the next room the gunshots died away, the hero smiled at the heroine, and Mr Pike, who was unusually old, thumped his empty glass on the table. The hairs on the back of Mr Moon's neck rose. 'I don't think he's from these parts, either,' he said.

10

WHEN Nameon returned to the cottage after narrowly avoiding Mr Moon, the fire he had lit before setting out was almost
dead. Even before the last tenants had deserted the cottage it
had been damp and in a state of decay. Now the fire had
brought the dampness to the surface, coaxing it from the
depths of walls and from the bits of furniture that had
survived both the weather and the pilfering. The armchair
which he had been using as a bed smelt of age and earth and
the walls were mildewed and crumbled when he stumbled
against them in the dark. Groping for the wood he had piled
up during the afternoon Nameon re-kindled the fire.

Outside the rain still fell but the wind that had driven into
his face with such hostility had dropped, and the cottage was
less draughty. Beyond the pieces of splintered glass that still
clung to the window-frames the clouds had thinned, and
through them drifted a dull, sickly coloured moon. He sat
down in the chair, too preoccupied to notice the woodlice
that surfaced with the dampness and that tumbled helplessly
on to the floor when he disturbed them. He decided to leave
within the hour, no matter how tired he was. Discarding his
rain-cloak, he pulled from a cupboard an overcoat and
proceeded to rip it down to something approaching his own
size. He left the sleeves and hem frayed and uneven but
checked the pockets for holes. He felt absurd wearing the
coat. It was damp and cumbersome but suited his needs. The

rest of his clothes he had been able to replace. His hat, his boots, a flaxen belt and the cloak he gathered in a pile, and when the fire was large enough he burnt them. But for a superior vest of green and red dragon skin (a possession he had no intention of disowning) he now had nothing to relate him to his own world except the few coins that had not fallen into the greedy hands of Mr Butler. From the same cupboard he took an umbrella, scattering spiders that had attempted to glue it to the wall with webs. He did not know what the umbrella was, but imagined it to be a weapon of kinds.

Glumly he studied the pigskin map and then pinned it into the inside pocket of his coat. He smothered the fire and left the cottage.

He walked what he thought to be due north, though he had no real way of telling, and often he deviated from his route to follow some easier sheep-track. He trudged along daydreaming of the relatively easy life he had led in Oakwood. Into his head he packed as many comforting images as possible, for they were a food of kinds, and they helped him forget the loneliness and bleakness of the moor. At eleven o'clock in the evening the clouds broke and the sheep-tracks swelled with rain. At one o'clock in the morning he still trudged along, and whenever he began to feel sorry for himself he fought off self-pity, knowing how useless such feelings are without a sympathetic ear to pour them into. By 2.30 he had arrived half-frozen at a farm.

Nameon crawled up a rough wooden ladder that rested against one of the outlying barns, and stumbling through the straw he collapsed into an exhausted sleep. He had put no more than seven miles between himself and Penmoor. For what remained of the night he slept dreamlessly, ignorant of the loud snoring and incoherent mumblings that issued from the throat of someone nearby, someone who had likewise needed a place to sleep and who had chosen the same barn.

*

Meanwhile, in the Drowned Duck, Mr Moon spent a much more comfortable evening. After he had extracted the relevant information from Mr Butler he sat in his room above the bar with his favourite book, *The Memoirs of Sherlock Holmes*. He was an avid reader and felt that no other character in fiction possessed as many enviable qualities as Mr Holmes. Solitary characters fascinated Mr Moon. Mirrored in them he saw bits and pieces of his own rather lonely existence. It was as if all the characters of whom he'd read were in reality pieces of a jigsaw, and that when the jigsaw was put together, lo and behold it was a picture of Mr Moon himself.

After two chapters of his book, Mr Moon placed it neatly on the bedside table and snuggled down between the crisp sheets to dream of snow and footprints, and of a quarry that was neither man nor animal.

The next morning he ate alone at a table covered by a white and blue checked cloth and decorated with a small bunch of snowdrops, still wet from the night's rain. He then settled his bill with Mr Butler and stepped out into the cobbled high street.

Even at this early hour – it was not yet eight – the day showed signs of being agreeable. Some streets away birds that had expected ice gossiped excitedly, and nearby a harnessed milk horse waited impatiently for a master who had disappeared. Beyond the streets the moor glistened. Above it floated a lake of mist and above the mist the moon was still visible.

Sitting in his motor car with the windows down Mr Moon studied his ordnance survey map. Around Penmoor he drew a circle, and within this circle pinpointed the most likely places where his quarry would shelter. Mr Moon reckoned the dwarf could be no more than a mile from the village for if, as Mr Butler had begrudgingly stated, the stranger had been

in the vicinity for several days, it was unlikely that he would take refuge far from the inn.

To the east the moor was broken by a crescent-shaped wood of beech trees and to the south was nothing but clumps of gorse, useless for sheltering even sheep. He discounted the western side of the village as it was the direction from which the dwarf had come, so this left him with the northern side where, scattered at random, stood several dilapidated cottages. It was these cottages Mr Moon decided to investigate.

Mr Moon found the cottage in which Nameon had been staying last of all. It took neither magnifying glass nor brilliant powers of deduction to guess it had been occupied very recently. The fender round the fire-place was still warm and scattered about the room were empty crisp packets, probably purchased at the Drowned Duck. There was even a wrapper from a pork pie stuffed clumsily down the side of a mouldy armchair. These things were evidence enough that the place had been used but they gave no clue as to what kind of person the occupant had been, so Mr Moon began a systematic examination. He discovered many separate piles of newspapers and magazines, which had obviously been in the cottage for years but which had only recently been sorted through. Because of the damp many were glued together, but care had been taken to prise them apart. One pile was opened at pictures of cities and machines, another at pictures of people, and others at photographs of animals. Why anyone should want to study these ordinary pictures puzzled Mr Moon. It seemed a rather silly thing for someone to spend their time doing in such a derelict place unless – and suddenly it was obvious – *unless they were not familiar with the world the pictures represented.*

Mr Moon searched the fire-grate and from between the charred wood and burnt rags he withdrew the sole of a small boot and the remains of a cloak. The inside of the cloak was lined with skin, but it was neither snake-skin nor leather. The figure that had jumped from the railway bridge in Brumble Head had been dressed oddly and this, thought Mr Moon, was what he had been wearing. He took the burnt cloth outside to see it better, and once in the light the scales on the lining glowed.

II

A̲t̲ eight in the morning the barking of a sheepdog woke
Nameon from the straw in which he had lain all night, soaked
and exhausted. For a moment he thought he was back home,
but then realizing where he was he buried himself deeper
beneath the straw and lay still, listening. Along with the
barking he could hear crows cawing, and the wind whistling
through the wooden frames of the barn. At first these were
the only sounds, and they did not frighten him. He relaxed
and was about to rise from the straw when a new sound
joined that of the crows and the wind. Not far from him
someone else was stirring. There was a yawn, a snort, and
then a polite cough. Nameon peeped through the straw.

Across the hayloft stood a tramp dressed in a black evening
suit. From one lapel hung a crumpled red carnation, the suit
was badly in need of repair. A white stubble of beard clung to
his face like frost, and on his feet was a pair of dancing
pumps.

   The tramp yawned again. He stretched and shook the
sleep from his head as if sleep were dust. Then strolling over
to the opening of the barn, he squatted down and looked
outside. 'It's a good day for once,' he said, 'the rain's
cleared.'

   Nameon said nothing. He sat up, his fists bunched
tightly. From the pocket of his suit the tramp took a pair of

pebble-lens spectacles and ceremoniously arranged them on his large beaky nose. Only when he was satisfied that the glasses fitted did he turn to face Nameon.

'Dumb?' he asked. 'Are you dumb?'

Nameon shook his head. The tramp shrugged. 'Suit yourself, sir,' he said. 'Some say nothing because they're dumb and others because they've nothing worth saying.'

Nameon tried to answer. He wanted to be civil, for the stranger seemed more friendly than harmful, but surprise had anchored down his tongue. All he could manage was a not very successful smile.

The stranger grunted, and returned to where he'd been sleeping. From the straw he unearthed a large suitcase and began to rummage inside it.

It was full of maps. Some were hand-drawn maps of islands on which were marked numerous crosses and dotted lines. Other maps were tiny, ripped from the pages of cheap diaries. There were maps of England and maps of India, world maps and maps of cities. There were even maps of underground railway stations and maps of the moon. Some were new, but most were old. The tramp took them from the case one by one, and held each against the light as if it were a photograph or portrait of some special friend. Some maps he stared at a long time, others barely merited a glance. Finally he selected a battered atlas of Britain, and returning the rest to the case he thumbed through it till he found the page he wanted.

From his pocket he produced a compass which he placed on the case beside the opened atlas. He referred from one to the other, quietly drumming his fingers on the corner of the page, as if indecisive about which direction to take. He finally closed the atlas and settled the matter by licking a finger and thrusting his hand out through the hayloft to discover which way the wind was blowing. Fascinated by the maps Nameon

54

edged nearer the tramp, and now stood at his side watching him go through what was obviously a daily ritual.

'It is the north wind,' said the tramp, 'and so I'll be going that way myself.' He pocketed the compass, sniffed, and returned the atlas to its case. 'D'you want to come?' he asked.

He seemed to find nothing odd about Nameon, though wrapped in his frayed coat and clutching his umbrella the dwarf looked the scruffiest and most bedraggled of creatures, and one would have thought that his appearance demanded some kind of explanation. But the tramp thought otherwise. He simply repeated his invitation, and before Nameon found words to reply the tramp was climbing awkwardly down from the loft clutching his suitcase tightly under one arm. Brushing the straw from his coat and making a futile effort to tidy himself up Nameon tumbled down after him.

The tramp was a tall, thin man, and his clothes, for all their absurdity, looked perfectly natural on him. 'You've decided to come along with me?' he asked.

'Yes,' said Nameon. 'But how far I go depends on a map.'

'A map? I thought I was the only one fond of maps.' The tramp stretched his hand down to the dwarf. 'Whoever you are, sir, you're welcome to travel along beside me. Any man who follows maps has my blessing and can be topped only by those who make them. My name is William O'Lovelife,' he said, 'and the horizon's my destination.'

And so it was that Nameon met someone who accepted him without question or comment. Mr O'Lovelife loved life. He was peppered with mad notions about the world, and in his own way was as much a stranger to it as Nameon. Beneath his arm he carried his battered case of maps and atlases, and he spoke with a voice that was both gentle and vague. He eulogized about the glories of the open road, about the stars and all the creatures that dwelt in either harmony or discord beneath them. He told, in snatches and out of

55

sequence, his own life-story, which seemed to Nameon too full to have been lived by a single man.

Nameon felt at home with Mr O'Lovelife. He hurried along at the tramp's side, travelling through country lanes and across open fields, and asking questions as openly and happily as if he were a child. Yet never once did he hint at the land from which he had come, and never once did Mr O'Lovelife inquire into his background, for backgrounds, said Mr O'Lovelife, are what most people who travel are travelling away from.

It was obvious to the tramp that Nameon was very much a stranger to the habits and manners of the world. His questions were simple, and it was without embarrassment that he took fright at such ordinary things as cows. He admitted to a fear of sheep and towards horses was more than a little apprehensive.

Though it was winter in the human world Nameon found the weather almost mild. He was used to near arctic conditions, for often as not Oakwood lay in silence beneath a film of frost. Yet even here the trees looked as if they would never grow leaves again, and in their branches, numb with cold, perched birds that had not had the sense to migrate. The shadows on the grass were black and long, the ploughed fields like brown and frozen waves. Whenever farmers saw the strangers they grinned and shook their heads, then went home to tell wives who never listened of the peculiar sight they'd seen.

The tall tramp in a ballroom suit and the raggy little bundle that trotted at his side paid little attention to those who passed near them. For the first time since waking on the Brumble Head lifeboat Nameon was enjoying his singular adventure, and he hurried in Mr O'Lovelife's wake gladly counting off the miles. Each step north was a step nearer home.

He was a most attentive listener, gleaning from his companion as many details about the world as the other felt fit to part with.

Because William O'Lovelife was a wanderer, the majority of the people he came into contact with – and they were not many – treated him with suspicion. To them the tramp seemed to have no origins, no roots with which they could identify. He lived happily without the things others lived for, and thus he made their daily struggles seem altogether pointless.

One day the travelling companions were climbing a path that wound round the brow of a hill and below them in the valley was a town dark with smoke and surrounded by untended fields. As they sat resting and staring down at the scene, Mr O'Lovelife went off into another of his poetic monologues.

'It's funny,' he said, 'how those who live in such places have come to look down their noses at the likes of me, as if they were richer and more proudly done by. They live in boxes, while I live in a mansion, the roof of which is filled with stars. Through this house the wind makes a pathway, and it is a pathway more reliable than any made by men. For books I read the signposts and for philosophics I have no time; they cannot make orchards blossom nor teach the birds new songs.'

Mr O'Lovelife nodded disapprovingly down at the little town and Nameon, who found it impossible to understand all he said, nevertheless nodded in agreement. The tramp spoke in a mass of clichés, his language borrowed at random from the books he had read as a child, but at least he lived out those clichés while others simply echoed them. He moved, spoke, gestured and breathed as if he knew for certain that behind the drab winter clouds a different kind of sky was waiting, and that beneath the exhausted and frost-bitten ground lurked every imaginable flower.

If Mr O'Lovelife had chosen to follow the ordinary roads, Nameon would have come into contact with towns much earlier than he did. But the tramp's obsession with old maps led him to follow roads and lanes that had become obsolete and all but vanished. Modern roads, he said, reflected modern times, and they smashed through the world rather than followed its natural contours. Thus their journey was slow, and between long silences the tramp found ample time to lecture Nameon and to explain how he had come to be leading the life he did.

12

'IN my youth,' said Mr O'Lovelife, 'I worked in a shipping
office as a book-keeper. While the paperwork piled up I sat
staring out the window my desk was fortunate enough to face.
Outside was a great river. It was busier then and thick with
traffic. And I wondered once too often to what lands those
ships went.

'I remember it was a fine June morning. During the eleven
o'clock tea-break I sneaked out of the office and signed up on a
steamer bound for America. Things were much simpler then.
I thought the ocean would last a life-time, but before three
years had passed I was land-sick and would lie in my bunk
dreaming of woods and grass, and the noise rain makes on
leaves, though, to tell the truth, it's not much different to the
noise it makes on tarpaulin.'

Mr O'Lovelife stopped and stared back down the road
along which they were tramping. 'Roads are funny,' he said.
'Not only do they lead away from places, but at one and the
same time they lead back towards them.

'I went back,' he said, 'and I tried to take up where I had
left off. I found another job as a book-keeper, but it didn't last
long. It was at the firm's annual ball that book-keeping and I
finally parted ways. I had tired of the music and the dancing,
and dressed as you see me now, in tailcoats and dancing
pumps, I strolled out on to the balcony to take the night air. I
was twenty-three years old then. I stood looking out at the
night, overawed by its vastness. I thought of mountains and

dawns, of deserts and fields that stretched on for ever, and suddenly I could not bear to be shut away from it all. Excusing myself on some pretext or other, I slipped out into the night. You might say that William O'Lovelife left the world of commerce, property, profit-and-loss during a ball, and has been dancing ever since.'

'But didn't you have to earn a living?' asked Nameon, thinking of the various jobs he'd done in Oakwood.

'A living? I did at first. It was a little later that I finally broke free. I remember I had a certain reluctancy to give myself wholly over to nature. I'd a fine singing voice, you see, and was putting it to good use. For a year or more I sang for my supper. I became known as "The Manchester Nightingale" and wandered daily down the centre of streets where more perambulators than motor cars were parked and where, on the roofs of houses, television aerials had not yet begun to fight pigeons for space.

'I sang mostly in bad weather, for I found that my songs, always sad, sounded even more melancholy in the rain. My favourite songs were sea-shanties and songs of parting, and my favourite day was Sunday.

'On Sundays people feeling pious and full of spuds would stumble out to place a sixpence in my hat – and those who could not come out themselves, those addicted to the warm hearths and radios, would send their children out to give me three pence, the theory being that three pence from a child was the same as six pence from a grown-up.'

Mr O'Lovelife rambled on in an almost jovial voice, but it seemed to Nameon that his flippant manner implied a less easy life than he would have him believe. His suit was threadbare and patched, and only from a distance did he seem at all elegant. For all his exuberance, O'Lovelife was old, and the atlases he carried under his arm were mirrored in his face, itself an atlas of kinds.

It would be untrue to say that Mr O'Lovelife and Nameon shared many adventures while tramping together. They were neither waylaid by thieves, nor did they meet with any monsters, nothing jumped out of bushes, and no wild motor cars or horses knocked them down. They discovered no strange objects and visited no lonely and haunted mansions. But for Nameon the experience was still colossal. He was overwhelmed by the size of things. He had never before seen large fields, he had never even seen a valley or a hill, and anything a great distance away he could not see at all, for his eyes were accustomed to a confined world. He considered passing within yards of two Guernsey cows adventure enough, and although he was continually being assured by Mr O'Lovelife as to their friendliness he was not convinced and stuck close to the side of his tall companion whenever it seemed they were mooing in a suspicious manner.

They followed the River Severn inland, sleeping when it grew too dark to travel and rising with the first light. They passed through Montgomeryshire, avoiding the main highways and tramping the smaller roads, roads that scarcely saw traffic and that passed through villages where Mr O'Lovelife usually obtained milk and bread. At a place called Forden they crossed and left the river behind them.

It was at Little Wenlock that Mr O'Lovelife 'borrowed' several apples from a meagre fruit display mounted outside a village grocery shop. Nameon said it seemed like stealing, but Mr O'Lovelife said it was his usual practice, and anyway he had been in the habit of taking apples from that particular stall for years. Mr O'Lovelife's reasoning was that the apples belonged to the trees in the first place, and so were already stolen by the time they arrived on the stalls. He did not sound very convincing, but the apples were the best Nameon had ever eaten.

On their last evening together they passed near Welshpool, where Mr O'Lovelife knew of a transport cafe, a place called Joe's, where everything was cheaper and better than anywhere else.

That afternoon the wintry sun disappeared and one large layer of cloud hung over the dull fields. Nameon's umbrella was useless and they were both soaked in a permanent drizzle. Mr O'Lovelife wrapped his case in plastic sheeting in order to keep his precious maps dry, and from the bits left over Nameon fashioned a hat. It was not a successful hat, the rain dripped from it on to the rest of his clothes, and the back of his overcoat became heavy and sodden. He started to complain about the unevenness of the ground and the amount of mud he was having to travel through.

'It's not so bad for tall people such as yourself,' he said without thinking, 'but for dwarfs and the like the going gets difficult. Our boots grow heavy and when the mud's squelchy we get stuck.'

It was doubtful whether the tramp heard Nameon, he was far too preoccupied with keeping his case dry. To all the dwarf's complaints he answered: 'You'll feel better when we reach Joe's,' or 'We'll be at Joe's soon,' as if the cafe of which he spoke was a refuge from the world's ills. He explained that at the cafe lorries sometimes stopped off on their way to Lewsbury market. 'If we're lucky we might get a lift and save a couple of days' tramping,' he said. 'I'm not one for riding the lorries myself, but when the weather's appalling I don't mind a bit of luxury.'

Nameon did not understand what Mr O'Lovelife meant by 'riding the lorries' and he felt a twinge of fear at the prospect. He thought that perhaps it was something all travellers did, and was sure he would be exposed as an impostor and lose the tramp's friendship when the moment to ride came. He was torn between explaining his identity to the tramp and prodding him for more information when suddenly Mr O'Lovelife said, 'There's Joe's now.'

13

THROUGH the drizzle Nameon saw a long wooden shack, set back from the road and lit by a stark white lamp. In front of the shack was a large open space where motionless lorries stood dripping with rain.

When the tramp opened the cafe door Nameon was prepared for neither the music nor the light that gushed out and assailed him. Panicking, he caught hold of Mr O'Lovelife's coat-tails and succeeded in bringing both of them crashing down in a confusion of hats, atlases and legs. They slid across a floor made wet by innumerable footprints till their journey was arrested by a jukebox.

Nameon had expected to find the interior of the cafe much the same as the Drowned Duck, a quiet place containing a few tables and fewer customers. But the place swarmed with giants. He had imagined all giants would look more or less the same, all variations on Mr and Mrs Butler and Mr O'Lovelife, but they were not. Some were tall and grossly fat while others were pale and undernourished and between these extremes were all manner of humans. They sat hunched morosely over tables or laughed and strolled through the cafe slapping one another on the back and shouting above the noise. The place smelled of humans and rain, and swirled with bright colours that in his own world were reserved for special occasions. They were as various as the gremlins, dwarfs and goblins of his own land. He

wondered how they could all be classified as 'humans'. He sat on the floor staring at them, as if at a canvas only a deranged goblin could paint.

A lorry-driver who had witnessed Nameon's panic and the ensuing tumble left his plate of egg and chips and came over to see if he could be of help. At his approach Nameon shrank deeper into his overcoat and clutched his umbrella in a vice-like grip.

'Is he ill, then?' the driver asked Mr O'Lovelife.

Having retrieved his priceless case, Mr O'Lovelife bent down at Nameon's side. The tramp took the dwarf's pulse and peered closely into his eyes. 'He's certainly frightened of something,' he said.

The lorry-driver glanced around the cafe. 'But there's nothing here to be frightened of.'

'Then it must be claustrophobia,' said Mr O'Lovelife.

'Eh?'

'Claustrophobia. It's the technical name for the affliction that has attacked my young friend here. Like myself he cannot stand being closed in by walls.'

The lorry-driver nodded. 'Like being locked in a lorry for ever,' he said. 'Eternally locked in a lorry cabin.'

'Yes, something like that,' agreed Mr O'Lovelife.

While the driver pondered sympathetically over how awful it would be to be locked for eternity inside a lorry, Mr O'Lovelife led Nameon to a corner table where he ordered sausage and chips twice and two cups of tea.

Until the meal arrived he sat thumbing through an atlas. With his index finger he traced his favourite journey, moving along motorways towards the broken lines that indicated ocean pathways. Within minutes he had travelled from England to Iceland and then, crossing the North Pole, passed down through Alaska and Canada into America. Here he stayed, smelling fields of ripened corn and wandering across the plains in search of buffalo. Next he pushed on into Mexico and here he dithered, daydreaming about the mysterious Inca tribes. Finally, adjusting his glasses and sniffing, Mr O'Lovelife travelled back across the Atlantic Ocean. After a long shuffle of pages, he returned to England. When the waitress arrived with the meal he had pocketed his glasses and was again staring absent-mindedly out of the misty window, his finger resting on a dot marked Welshpool. It had been a long journey.

So that he would not have to watch Mr O'Lovelife or look at the waitress Nameon followed suit, and taking out his own map he stared at it helplessly. His brain was too conscious of his surroundings to be able to concentrate, and even if he had been able to it would have been quite pointless, for north was north, no matter which way one looked at it, and only when he was well into the north would the map be of any use.

When the waitress finished fussing about their table and left, they both put away their maps and began to eat.

It was Nameon's first real meal. So far he had lived on apples, frost-blighted carrots and rather suspect sandwiches which Mr O'Lovelife had produced from his overcoat pocket with a flourish. Nameon ate with his fingers, and was pleased to discover that the chips were in fact potatoes and the sausage a kind of meat. Tea was not to his liking, but he found that when drowned in sugar it became tolerable. Both in eating and drinking he made loud noises which, if not for the constant music blaring out of the jukebox, might have attracted considerable attention. Mr O'Lovelife ignored the manners of his guest. Though he himself ate in a fashion befitting his status as a gentleman, he had come into contact with such a variety of people that he no longer found anyone's eating habits extraordinary.

The meal would have been delicious had it not been for Nameon's nagging suspicion that all was not well. He was not worried about being watched – although everyone in the cafe was conscious of his size they were polite enough not to stare – but he found himself growing more and more impatient with Mr O'Lovelife. It had become obvious to him that the tramp was in no hurry to go anywhere and he found this irritating. The tramp's lack of impatience increased his own to such an extent that he wanted to leave the cafe and get back on the road immediately. Yet he hesitated, uncertain how to set about leaving his companion, and even ashamed that he wanted to. He pushed away his half-empty plate and climbed down from his seat, but the tramp restrained him.

'There's no need to be in such a curfuffle,' he said. 'Sit down and tell me about your map.'

It was obvious that Mr O'Lovelife had been thinking of nothing else throughout the meal, and that he could no longer contain his curiosity. Nameon took the map from his pocket again. 'It's a map of your world,' he said, no longer bothering with caution.

'And are there maps of other worlds?' asked Mr O'Lovelife. 'Here, let me have a look.'

He took the map from Nameon and examined it. 'It's splendid,' he said. 'And the first I've ever seen copied on to pigskin.'

'Is it accurate though?' asked Nameon. His voice was thin, for it was a question he hardly dared ask. One of his major fears was that Greenweed's map was inexact.

Mr O'Lovelife gave the map a scholarly glance. 'It would have been perfectly accurate a few hundred years ago,' he said.

To Nameon a couple of hundred years was neither here nor there. He knelt up on his chair, and leaning across the table jabbed the map with his finger. 'What about this area?' he asked. 'Surely nothing much would have changed here?'

He was pointing to the crosses that indicated where the oak trees stood.

'Ah, that's in Northumberland,' said Mr O'Lovelife, turning the map. 'It used to be lovely up there.'

'You mean it has changed?' asked Nameon incredulously.

'In parts it's well changed. Look here.' He took a pen from his case and before Nameon could stop him, started altering the map. Where fields were indicated he drew towns, and near the crosses Greenweed had made he drew hotels and amusement arcades. 'Now this place,' he said, referring to somewhere called Holtwood, 'doesn't actually exist, or at least not on any map I know, and if you want to get where the crosses are, you'll do best to remember it's called Norton Bay.' With a quick flourish of the pen Mr O'Lovelife transformed Nameon's ancient map. Towns, cities, and motorways blossomed, forests vanished, names changed and only rivers and coastlines remained intact. 'The place you want is called Norton Bay now, not Holtwood. That place doesn't exist any more.'

When he gave back the map it was no longer a picturesque diagram but a jumbled and complicated mess. Nameon was bewildered, but relieved that he could now rely on it, not being much concerned anyway with its aesthetic value.

The map certainly looked gloomy. What he had begun to anticipate as a pleasant journey through dales and woodlands he now saw was to be a long trudge through areas that crawled with human beings. The prospect disheartened him. 'I was right to feel impatient,' he thought. 'I've been moving at the speed of a snail.'

'I've got to go,' he told Mr O'Lovelife. 'I've got to leave immediately.'

To his surprise the tramp did not try to dissuade him.

'Let me try and get you a lift into the next main town,' he said. 'From there you can head up towards Steelborough, then branch out towards the coast. It'll take time, and if time is what you haven't got then from Steelborough a train will take you to Norton Bay. Stay here a moment.'

Mr O'Lovelife left Nameon at the table and approached a group of men on the far side of the room. He asked a question but they shook their heads and pointed to the lorry-driver who had offered to help Nameon up off the floor. When Mr O'Lovelife spoke to him the driver nodded and smiled.

The tramp came back. 'I've got you a lift,' he told Nameon. 'No one else seems to be going any farther north tonight but Paddy says he can drop you at Lewsbury. It's on the way.'

Minutes later the driver came over to their table and informed them he was ready to go. Nameon made sure the map was securely pinned into his pocket. He wanted to thank Mr O'Lovelife, but the tramp neither expected nor welcomed gratitude. Nameon slid from his seat and followed Paddy across the room. At the doorway he stopped. Mr O'Lovelife seemed already to have forgotten him and was staring blankly into the air, nursing his case on his lap. 'Till the leaves reopen, then,' he called. But his voice was drowned by the music from the jukebox and the tramp did not hear him. Mr O'Lovelife knew he would never meet the dwarf again, there were far too many roads down which people had to travel alone.

14

Mr Moon was still searching for Nameon.

When he returned to the car he had parked not far from the derelict cottage, the ex-detective found curled up on the passenger seat a rather dishevelled dog. Its ears were large and out of proportion to the rest of its body, which was small. Unlike most strays, it showed no signs of starvation. It snored contentedly, one paw flopped over a large, well-chewed bone. Mr Moon tried to wake the dog. He shook it gently and then he shook it roughly, but the creature seemed in no hurry to move, being perfectly content where it was. Mr Moon knew the dog was awake. When he first shook it it had opened one eye and, glancing through a mass of matted curls, seen Mr Moon, guessed him harmless, and resumed its snoring. It had, however, placed its paws more firmly over its bone.

Mr Moon took an instant liking to the mongrel and decided to leave it curled up on the seat for the time being. The time being stretched into days.

The nearest inhabited place to the cottage in which the dwarf had first sheltered was Bracken Farm, seven miles away across the moor. When Mr Moon arrived there and discreetly inquired whether any odd-looking person had been seen in the vicinity, the farmer, who looked not unlike the bulls he bred, said no, but that he suspected one of his hay lofts had recently been slept in by a couple of tramps. Mr

Moon discounted the possibility of his quarry being one of the vagrants, for it seemed unlikely to him that the dwarf would seek company.

He spent nearly a week combing the area. With the dog he travelled on foot to places inaccessible by road. He travelled across fields and hills, his boots thick with mud, his hands and face raw from the cold. A cold sore appeared on his mouth, and chilblains on his feet. He made inquiries at numerous farms and in villages, but nobody seemed to know anything about the 'dwarf'. He was sometimes recognized by people who had seen him on television, and thinking him an idiot they humoured him, bolstering up his hopes with inventions that inevitably led to disappointment.

The dog seemed to share his disappointment. It had obviously been without an owner a long time. It wore no collar and answered to whatever name was called. Mr Moon decided, more for his own benefit than the dog's, to call it Wanderlust. It was an appropriate enough name. Wanderlust was curious. He was preoccupied with rabbit-holes and ditches, and would even turn stones with his paw to study the insects living beneath them. He investigated places he should not investigate. In backyards he terrified ducks and tried to make friends with chickens and chased cats. He seemed to have a built-in radar system that led directly to bones. He was never without them and some, Mr Moon felt sure, were found on kitchen tables rather than in fields.

Then one evening early on in his search, Mr Moon had a stroke of luck. He put up at the Ragbone Hotel.

Despite its name the Ragbone did not allow dogs inside, but this did not bother Wanderlust, who was adept at sneaking through doors unnoticed. It was a drab and humourless place, and the proprietors were the thinnest, boniest couple Mr Moon had set eyes upon. On entering the hotel he resigned himself to a dull and uneventful evening, but it was here he found the information he had been searching for in vain.

Sipping a cup of tea in the residents' lounge, Mr Moon could not help but overhear a conversation between two fellow guests and the proprietress. His ears pricked up immediately, and he sat motionless, the teacup poised between his mouth and his knees.

'. . . It was the funniest sight we've seen in a long time,' exclaimed the first guest. 'They were walking in the meadow behind Mingers Farm. There was a lanky tramp dressed up like Lord Muck, tails'n'all, and another wrapped up like a parcel.'

'But that wasn't all,' said his friend, 'it was the disparity in sizes.'

'I was coming to that bit,' said the first. 'The small one was a right Tom Thumb, no bigger than a child. But his face, now his face looked very old.'

'It was a young face,' contradicted his friend.

'It was old and battered,' said the first.

'Battered and young,' said the other. 'I saw him clearly.'

'And so did I, and I say it was the face of a goblin.'

Both men agreed on this last statement.

'I heard from someone they'd been stealing apples from Mrs Wilkie's shop up in Little Wenlock,' volunteered the proprietress. 'Not that Mrs Wilkie would mind, that woman has no business sense whatsoever. She'd let the devil steal her apples if he looked hungry enough.'

Their conversation then drifted off in a direction Mr Moon had no wish to follow. Back up in his room he studied his map, and with a pencil traced out the route he thought the tramps were taking. He was convinced that one must be the dwarf, and that his theory about the creature wanting to avoid company was wrong. This upset Mr Moon, for he took pride in what he called his 'Holmesian deductions' and was quite shaken when they failed him.

He was now obsessed with the dwarf. It wandered nightly through his dreams, which were always the same. In them Mr Moon was being chased by a figure holding a scythe, and was running across fields that ended abruptly at the ocean's edge. His lungs hurt with the effort of running but the dwarf beckoned him on, urging him to run faster and faster. In its hand the dwarf held a tattered map, but whenever Mr Moon reached for it a gust of wind blew it away and it went flurrying across the sand like an injured gull.

It was morning and it was thundering. The gust of wind heard in his dream he heard again. It rattled the window-frames and smashed rain against the glass. Mr Moon sat up in the bed, his bones aching. The room smelt musty, the eiderdown was stained and moth-eaten, the wallpaper a drab grey. In the street below, Wanderlust was sniffing the wheels of the motor car. Once again Mr Moon packed his bags. Once again he paid his bill for the night's lodging. With Wanderlust he set out towards Little Wenlock in search of the grocery store he had heard mentioned in the previous evening's conversation.

He arrived in the village before midday. The drive had been easy, the roads deserted. Rain had kept people inside their houses and only a few were hurrying down the streets, women with canvas shopping bags and children in plastic mackintoshes who skipped and slid on the cobbled roads.

Mrs Wilkie's grocery store was the first shop over a small humped bridge. The wooden display counter that was per-manently fixed outside the shop had been cleared because of the rain, and Mrs Wilkie herself sat reading a magazine behind the shop window. She looked up when Mr Moon parked his motor and rushed across the pavement into the shop. She was bored sitting among the spuds and carrots, and was glad of some diversion from her magazine.

Yes, she said, two peculiar tramps had passed the shop recently and one was known to her as Mr O'Lovelife, but the other was a stranger and had hovered farther away from the shop. Mr O'Lovelife, she said, had stopped outside the shop in order to purloin a couple of apples. 'He does it every year, every year without fail he comes through Little Wenlock, regular as the marigolds. And he always steals apples and he always looks the same. He always looks old and always carries a case under his arm. In thirty years I've seen him as many times and it seems that only the case gets any older. No one knows what's inside it.'

Mrs Wilkie stared out the window at the rain. 'I hear say it's full of money,' she said, 'but I don't believe it. What would he be doing tramping the length and breadth of the country, if it were? No, I think he keeps something in his suitcase that's far more precious to him than money.'

'And does he always travel with a companion?' asked Mr Moon.

'It's the first time O'Lovelife's been seen with anyone,' she said, 'but I'm glad he's found a friend at last. I've never seen two so opposite. It seems only right he should take a fancy to someone so small and bizarre.'

'Bizarre? Then you saw him closely?'

'He stayed on the far side of the road. But that was near enough to tell he wasn't, well, *normal* if you know what I mean.'

Mr Moon knew exactly what she meant. 'Have you any idea where they've gone?' he asked.

'Maybe Joe's.'

'Joe's?'

'A transport cafe near Welshpool,' sighed Mrs Wilkie, as if he ought to have known. 'Paddy often drives up that way delivering spuds.'

'Paddy?'

'My husband. He often drives up that way, and he's often seen Mr O'Lovelife at the cafe.'

Mrs Wilkie turned her attention back to the rain. A child trailing a broken kite was hurrying across the bridge.

Mr Moon thanked her and scribbling down the address of the cafe he returned to the motor car. He believed his determination was at last paying off. He reversed into a side street near the fruit shop and happily turned the car back over the bridge, taking the left fork on to what he thought was the Welshpool road. But unfortunately it was quite a different road; and Mr Moon drove off in completely the wrong direction.

15

PADDY the long-distance lorry-driver was a huge Irishman. A giant by any standards, he could hardly squeeze himself into the lorry. He was a staunch believer in all things Irish, though he had lived the best part of his life in Wales where years ago he had loved and married Mrs Wilkie. He believed in leprechauns, in pots of gold beneath rainbows, and that he would one day win the football pools as surely as Shamrock Rovers would win the World Cup. He had driven lorry-loads of potatoes between Little Wenlock and Lewsbury Market for the last thirteen and a half years.

Nameon found riding the lorries very agreeable and not at all what he had expected. The cab was the warmest place he had ever been in, so warm, in fact, that his clothes had begun to steam and smell rather peculiar. Paddy did not mind the smell. He was continually munching sweets and sausage rolls and sipping from a large bottle he kept at the back of the cab, and which he occasionally offered to Nameon. Sitting there, full of sausages, chips, sherbet lemons and cider, Nameon felt drowsy and perfectly content. His fears vanished. Come what may, the human world was proving not such a bad place after all. He yawned. He would travel up to – where was it? – Norton, as fast as he could, for he could travel no faster than that. And then Nameon dozed off, and when he woke Paddy was talking about leprechauns.

'. . . bit smaller than yourself, if you don't mind me saying.

76

It was years ago now. I was six or seven and it was sitting in full view, if you please, on top of the Bally Copland Windmill. There was quite a crowd gathered round it, and this man called Fallon, a highly respected chap in those parts, got the army to fly over it in a helicopter and take pictures. I tried to catch it myself, but it was no use. They've got magic powers, you see. I suppose it could have changed me into a bullfrog had it wanted. Ah, but I was young then. Young and reckless. Then another time . . .'

Paddy droned on and the lorry droned on, and it was a battle between them as to who made the most noise. Nameon was amazed at Paddy's misconception and he dozed off again, wishing that like Paddy's mad leprechaun he too had the power to turn people into frogs. How simple life would be if all one had to do for a bit of peace was to wave a wand and change people into frogs. He imagined his own world and the human world, with all their worries and disasters, reduced to a marshland in which frogs jumped and croaked and over which he was the sole master. How lovely and simple it would be, he thought, if magic were so mundane. He dreamt he was sitting at the forest's edge mumbling spells that did all his work for him, while his friends looked on with admiration.

Then Paddy's voice woke him again. The dials in the cab glowed, showing the miles that had vanished. It was after four o'clock in the morning. The lorry rumbled through sleepy villages, through Mayden and Chilbury, Worthen and Westbury, passing tiny cottages and sprawling farms. The windscreen wipers chased each other across the glass, pushing away the persistent rain. Nameon crouched on the gear-box, bleary-eyed and fascinated by the way the lorry's headlamps lit up the roadside, illuminating and transfiguring the simplest things till the night through which they sped seemed alive with demons.

Paddy talked endlessly. He talked about the various wars

that were in progress, and about the price of eggs; he talked about the places he had been and the places he intended to go. Finally he talked about himself, and upon this topic spoke lovingly and at length.

They were thundering through a housing estate when Paddy nudged Nameon, who had dozed off again, to point it out. The estate was made up of towers and was immense, it had obliterated acres of rich farmland, and been dreamt up by a gang of businessmen one evening over dinner. Nameon's story-stones had spoken of such towers. He had read many traditional tales in which harmless giants had been walled up within them, doomed for ever to wander down corridors or to live in tiny, comfortless rooms. These awesome towers seemed to subdue Paddy, for as he drove between them he became silent.

At 6.40 in the morning the lorry arrived in Lewsbury.

The market-place was in a square at the foot of a rather impressive building that had once been both the Town Hall and the Corn Exchange. The commercial centre of the town had long since shifted, and the building was left behind, now a place in which to store barrows, awnings and crates of non-perishable goods. The market swarmed with an odd assortment of people. There were neatly dressed young men buying bulk loads for supermarket chains and farmers standing uncomfortably in tweed suits worn only on market days. Women hurried about beneath umbrellas seeking out the fattest chickens and the cheapest lambs while the market workers zigzagged between them on important errands.

Paddy manoeuvred his lorry among the stalls until he found the one to which he was supposed to deliver his potatoes. When he left the lorry to supervise the unloading Nameon had no idea what to do. He sat in the cab looking out of the window. As far as the eye could see was a mass of stalls, and barrows loaded with apples and potatoes jostled with barrow-loads of plums and nursery flowers. Skinned rabbits hung on hooks beside stalls glowing with oranges, butchered cows hung beside milk churns and stalls piled high with cheeses, and the whole scene was lit with kerosene lamps and electric bulbs strung on makeshift cables, for though it was morning it was still frosty and dark.

It was an unruly mixture between a blood-bath and harvest festival. Tearing his eyes away from the overpowering scene, Nameon busied himself. He took off his boots and replaced the soaked paper in them with folded magazines from the back of the cab, using the old paper to clean the mud from his trouser legs. After this feeble effort to make himself presentable he checked that his map was secure, then lowered himself out of the lorry and down into the fruit-splattered square.

From the cabin he had been able to see Paddy standing beside a makeshift tea-stall. Paddy had beckoned to him, but once Nameon reached the ground his panoramic view was no longer available. He was engulfed in a sea of human beings. He worked his way between an assortment of massive crates and baskets in what he supposed was Paddy's direction, but on coming to where the tea-stall ought to have been he found only more crates. In no time at all he was lost among them, he was adrift, swept along by the bustle of the market. He soon gave up hope of ever rediscovering Paddy. He found coffee- and tea-stalls by the dozen, and lorries identical to the one he had ridden, but of the talkative Irishman there was no trace. He pushed his way timidly between the towering crowd until he came upon the building he had seen while entering the market. Climbing the impressive steps of the Corn Exchange he was once more able to see the scene in its entirety. He wondered what to do next, but no immediate plan came to mind. He sat down on the steps, and felt very lost.

Within hours the market was over. The morning had crept up and shooed it away. The crowds and the lorries departed, the stalls and awnings were dismantled and packed. Now other men came into the square, bent and grey and clutching brooms. They swept purple paper, bruised fruit, and the stumps of lettuces into piles. Like Nameon they were dressed in large ill-fitting coats and wore thick boots. Their faces were red and thick with sleep, and their pockets bulged with possessions. Around them gathered an army of birds as bedraggled as themselves.

Although he felt home-sick Nameon decided that with so many miles conquered he could delay his journey and explore at least a little of the town. Its energy excited him. After providing himself with damaged fruit, he set off, experimenting first by sitting in parks on remote benches where he felt safest. Occasionally a solitary human being would pass and Nameon would munch at an apple or bow his head and pretend to be asleep.

When he grew tired of the park Nameon continued his exploration in the streets, stopping briefly to look up from the pavements and catch glimpses of the surrounding buildings. It was the shop windows that really intrigued him, but the streets where these were most numerous were crowded. He was seldom lucky enough to find a street that contained lots of shop windows but only a few people. The shop that fascinated him most was a clothes store. On first passing it Nameon had not believed the evidence of his eyes. It both drew and repelled him. The second and third times he passed the window its contents still dismayed him. It was full of embalmed bodies, draped in lengths of cloth. Nameon shuddered, glad that such barbaric practices did not exist in his own world.

Keeping to the least occupied roads the dwarf eventually found himself in the oldest area of the town, among narrow streets of Tudor houses lined with peeling window-boxes and tubs of blighted geraniums. One such street led to a massive fortification into the walls of which were carved heads of demons, angels and other supernatural creatures.

It was Lewsbury Cathedral.

16

THE cathedral was surrounded by lawns on which ancient gravestones had been scattered in a decorative manner that seemed to have little or nothing to do with the solemnity of death. Nameon stood gazing at it, his hands sunk deep into the vast pockets of his overcoat. The plastic hat he had made while with Mr O'Lovelife and his umbrella he had left in Paddy's lorry.

Trying to look invisible seemed to have worked. With a few exceptions the people he passed in the streets had shown no curiosity, and the exceptions had all been children.

The newspapers had long dropped their leprechaun story, but it was still a major topic of conversation in the playgrounds. Johnny Plackham, who had been the first to protest against the way newspapers had demeaned the leprechaun, had done his best to keep the creature alive in the minds of children.

In every village and town in the land at least one child had reported sighting the creature, and in major cities reports of sightings were commonplace. Ninety-nine per cent of these reports were false alarms, but still the rumours spread rapidly and with astonishing ease. Brief telephone calls sneaked while parents were absent and letters to cousins a hundred miles away all boasted of meetings and hinted at more complicated involvements with the creature. Sometimes the rumours suggested two leprechauns were abroad, even three. Arguments also raged as to whether it was even a leprechaun at all. Why not a goblin, some said, or a dwarf?

Nameon, ignorant as to the extent of his fame, walked down the pathway to investigate the cathedral.

It was a day to be remembered in Lewsbury Cathedral, at least it was for Daphne Dawling and Rodney Ruskin. Rodney was a verger at the cathedral and Miss Dawling simply liked being inside it. She lived off bread, baked beans, sweets and sometimes soup, and slept in a hostel run by the church for those who had not been able to cope with the demands society made of them. She was simple and good, and she prayed audibly and avidly, and much too loudly for the likes of Rodney Ruskin. When Miss Dawling lifted her voice to God she lifted it, and it was useless suggesting to her that she could pray quietly and still be heard with ease by the Almighty. She was a source of constant distress to Rodney Ruskin, and posed problems he found impossible to solve without injuring either his conscience or that of the church.

Most people visited Lewsbury Cathedral to see its beautiful stained-glass windows and to gape at its imposing architecture, but Miss Dawling came to praise Him for whom the place was originally built. When there was singing in the cathedral, and when it proved impossible to keep her away, Miss Dawling's voice could be heard above the rest. One might have said her voice soared like a lark, but if a toad could have soared then that would have been a more appropriate description. Her voice was rough, it was awkward and flat, and plain as the clothes she wore.

Her habit of leaving sweet-wrappers and breadcrumbs among the pews gave Rodney a reason for having her dismissed, but she would return within the hour and was so obviously a lamb of God that he had neither the courage nor heart to dismiss her twice in one day. With the Dean's blessing Rodney Ruskin had once offered her a side room in which to sing and pray, a room in which choir-boys' surplices and other paraphernalia were stored, but Miss Dawling was obstinate in her refusal to be moved from the main body of the cathedral.

Rodney Ruskin did not pray often, and his singing was hardly above a whisper, but he too loved the cathedral. It was not so much the solemn beauty of the place, but the little jobs he performed amongst that beauty. He loved arranging the bibles in neat rows and polishing the silver candlesticks. He loved dusting the statues and locking the doors at night and opening them early in the morning when the cathedral lawns were still wet with dew and nobody was about. Next to God's, it was Rodney's cathedral, or so he thought. It was not the Archbishop's, nor the Dean's, not the priests', nor curates', nor the rich families', who had bought nameplates for their pews, but Rodney Ruskin's. He loved the place with a secular love, while Miss Dawling's love was passionate.

When Nameon pushed open the gigantic doors and stepped spellbound into the cathedral, Miss Dawling was praying near the altar and Rodney was polishing candlesticks in a side chapel.

Nameon crept into an alcove and, safely hidden among the shadows, gaped about him. Motes of dust floated through pallid sunbeams and in the windows drifted figures of a colour and brilliance he had never imagined. The figures quavered, changing hues as clouds passed by outside. He realized his dreams had been dull in comparison with the reality that now eclipsed them. The building overawed him, the reasons for its splendour were beyond him, for Nameon knew nothing about God. His own gods were the spirits of the forest; they lived in the remotest possible trees and in the bodies of great owls, and the single place raised in their honour in Oakwood was a small, unimposing mound of stones that stood half-hidden at the forest's edge.

The sound of someone mumbling quietly caught his attention. He ventured out of the alcove and deeper into the church where, in a front pew, he spied Miss Dawling. Nameon wondered what she was doing, and in his efforts to creep forward for a closer look knocked over a pile of prayer books Mr Ruskin had recently stacked. They came crashing down with a loud, echoing thud. At that exact moment the cathedral doors swung open and in wandered a group of schoolchildren, led by a harassed-looking schoolmaster.

Miss Dawling knew the noise had been made by something other than the doors being opened, but her attention was momentarily distracted and Nameon took the opportunity to dive into another alcove.

Things might have turned out differently had not Miss Dawling been praying for a sign when the prayer books came toppling down. She did not know exactly what kind of sign she had been praying for. Such details did not bother her.

While the schoolchildren were being herded into a group at the far end of the cathedral, Miss Dawling explored the shadows among which the books had fallen. Thus while the schoolmaster droned on about wars and kings and panes of glass, Miss Dawling crawled about the flagstones on her hands and knees, offering the children an entertaining diversion from their history lesson.

Satisfied there was nobody among the benches who could have toppled the books she turned next to the alcoves.

A few were occupied by saints, the rest by marble angels. One statue considered more important than the rest was the statue of the Angel of Mercy. It had been specially commissioned by the Archbishop himself and was enclosed by a row of iron railings. Miss Dawling was half-way over these railings when Mr Ruskin appeared holding a candlestick and polishing rag.

'Miss Dawling!' he hissed.

Miss Dawling froze, one leg suspended in the air, as if practising some difficult ballet movement. She knew that, somehow, climbing into this particular alcove was as bad if not worse than leaving sweet-wrappers and breadcrumbs among the pews.

'What on earth are you doing?' he asked.

Miss Dawling sniffed. 'I am taking a closer look at the statue, Mr Ruskin.'

'But you can see it perfectly well from this side of the railings,' complained the verger.

'It's not actually the statue I want to see. I want to see if there is anything in the alcove with the angel, Mr Ruskin.'

'With the angel?' Mr Ruskin peered at the statue. The angel was made of a particularly white marble and it glowed in the shadows, but the alcove was not so dark that the back wall could not be seen. Mr Ruskin stared hard, his eyes covering every inch of the wall.

'There's nothing in there but the angel,' he said.

'There must be,' said Miss Dawling. 'The other alcoves are empty.'

'And why should this one be any different?'

Miss Dawling did not feel inclined to give an explanation. 'I've just got to make sure,' she whispered. 'It's important, Mr Ruskin.'

'Well, I'm afraid that I shall have to forbid it,' said the verger more sternly that he intended to. 'That angel has railings around it for the express purpose of keeping people from touching it. The world, Miss Dawling, is full of statues that have been worn away by irresponsible fingers.'

Nameon, crouching behind the angel, sighed with relief. It was only the tiniest sigh, but unfortunately the alcove

86

produced an echo that was distinctly audible. Because of the echo the sigh seemed to come not from behind the angel, but from the angel itself.

'Good grief,' exclaimed Rodney Ruskin, 'that was a sigh.'

'No,' said Miss Dawling, 'it was a sign.'

'A what . . . ?'

'A sign.'

While Miss Dawling explained what had happened an authoritative voice behind them droned on oblivious of the drama. 'And now this last statue', said the schoolteacher, 'is the Angel of Mercy, a work specially commissioned for Lewsbury by Archbishop Stowford in 1953 and executed by Sir Arthur Penny. It is immensely valuable and is –'

'Worth Arthur Million,' muttered a bored and anonymous voice.

The children sniggered but the teacher, unable to appreciate the pun, demanded silence.

Rodney Ruskin and Miss Dawling were too engrossed to notice the crowd gathering around them. 'It's the first time it's done that,' said the verger turning pale.

Sensing the presence of more people Nameon groaned again. Again it was only the tiniest sound, but it echoed from the walls and it seemed for all the world as if the Angel itself was groaning.

Miss Dawling fainted. She fell in a dramatic swoon into the arms of the schoolteacher. The teacher, Mr Sidney Rabbitt, did not know what to do with the body he found himself clutching. It was Mr Ruskin who took the initiative. He also took Miss Dawling's feet.

'What's the matter with her?' asked Mr Rabbitt.

'What's the matter? It ought to be obvious. She's fainted, that's what.'

Rodney Ruskin was in such a hurry to get away from the statue and out into the open that he almost pulled Miss

Dawling out of the teacher's arms. He was convinced the sound was caused by natural phenomena, but he too felt faint and in need of fresh air.

Immediately they had gone the boys crowded round the alcove to conduct their own investigation. The strain of hiding and waiting to be caught proved too much for Nameon and he came out from behind the angel.

When he appeared the children froze. They stood facing each other through the railings. Nameon stared at them, searching for a gap in case he had to fight through them to escape. There was no need. In their faces he saw surprise, not aggression. The hush was broken as suddenly as it had fallen and the boys began chattering as one. They crowded together, and after a few hurried conversations and several arguments, one of the group stepped forward, and with an expression that suited the importance of the occasion said stiffly: 'I am Benjamin Platts, a lieutenant of SPLOT. We recognize you and are sworn to help. You are among friends.'

Nameon remembered the reporter he had seen in the crystal at Mrs Butler's inn, and how the reporter had spoken about the children forming a society for his protection. It occurred to him that perhaps the crystal had forecast this meeting, but he had not been able to interpret its message.

He was embarrassed by the awe in which the children seemed to hold him, but decided for the time being he could do nothing better than to leave himself in their hands. Crowding round him they hustled Nameon out of the cathedral and into the back of the school-bus. Here they interrogated him, asking endless questions about the world he had come from.

But the dwarf wanted to relate his adventures since arriving in the human world, and even when it became obvious that they thought the human world of little consequence he persisted.

Mr Moon's brief appearance on television had been discussed extensively, and in the children's minds the poor man had assumed the status of arch-villain. Nameon used this to his advantage, and promising to talk about Oakwood later, he elaborated on the Drowned Duck episode, letting them believe he had been caught by Mr Moon but after a terrible fight had escaped. The early morning rambles through the countryside with Mr O'Lovelife became a nightmarish hunt through marshlands, in which he and the tramp were pursued by howling dogs. Such elaborations came easily to Nameon, for it was his habit of daydreaming and his vivid imagination that had caused him to go poking about in Greenweed's boat in the first place.

Out on the cathedral's cold lawns Miss Dawling soon recovered and, leaving her in the capable hands of Rodney Ruskin, Mr Rabbitt hurriedly returned to the school-bus. He counted the children to make sure none had been left behind and after complaining about the untidy heap of coats piled up on the back seat he started for home.

The children had decided on a plan of action. It was Nameon's good fortune that they were going to Steelborough, and Steelborough, besides being a place from which Nameon could catch a train farther north, was also the home of the famed but secretive Johnny Plackham, the leader of SPLOT.

The plan was simple: Nameon was to be dropped on the outskirts of Steelborough when the bus arrived later that day. Previous experience had shown Mr Rabbitt to be in the habit of stopping on the outskirts of the city and leaving the children alone on the bus while he attended to business. As he inevitably stopped outside the Half Way public house, 'attending to business' meant he was popping in for a drink. This would give Nameon a chance to slip from the bus undetected.

After dumping Nameon, Benjamin Platts was to contact Johnny Plackham who would then come and collect Nameon. The plan sounded very simple, but as an extra safeguard Nameon was told to memorize Johnny's address. He pointed out that it would be easier to have the address written down on a piece of paper, but the children were bent on making things as secretive as possible.

'Tell us more about Mr Moon,' they said. 'Do you think he wants to kill you?'

Nameon recoiled at the thought. 'I don't think he wants to do anything quite as beastly as that,' he said.

'But you can never be sure,' said the children.

17

WHEN he had first seen the small figure on the bridge in Brumble Head Mr Moon had been a neatly dressed and rather quiet man, resigned to spending the remainder of his days in modest retirement. But his obsession with Nameon had changed him.

In his various hotel beds Mr Moon tossed and turned. All night he coughed and all day seemed out of breath. He no longer shaved and the stubble on his chin had grown thick and grey. Buttons hung off his clothes and his trousers were held up by string, his braces having got lost in one of the numerous rooms in which he'd stayed. Any friend chancing to meet him would have remarked on his appearance and shown concern for his health. Mr Moon was not well enough to live the kind of life he was now leading. A cold caught while standing on Brumble Head bridge was worse and his health was rapidly deteriorating, but if anyone had suggested he give up his absurd hunt and return home he would have refused. Though apprehensive about the content of the note he had been given by his doctor he was resolute in his determination to find the dwarf.

The rain had been falling in such torrents and his windscreen wipers working so poorly that when Mr Moon left Mrs Wilkie's shop he took no notice of the signposts he passed and arrived in Oswestry, a market town specializing in cattle and transport cafes, thinking it was Welshpool. He visited five cafes asking if they were ever frequented by a man called O'Lovelife before discovering he was in the wrong town. It was too late to travel any more that night and so he stayed on in Oswestry.

The next evening he found the right cafe. The rain seemed to have followed him. He parked his car and with Wanderlust at his heels ran through the downpour. If he had not kept his head bowed against the rain his search might have ended there and then, for at the very moment Mr Moon was crossing the forecourt, Nameon was being helped into the lorry bound for Lewsbury.

Sighing with a mixture of relief and exhaustion Mr Moon flopped down into the nearest empty chair, and Wanderlust scrambled beneath. He picked up a hand-written menu but rain dripping from his hat obliterated the writing. Not that it mattered. He had eaten in so many transport cafes that he knew their menus by heart, and when the waitress appeared he ordered steak and kidney pie, sprouts and potatoes for himself, and a bone for Wanderlust. The pie was delicious and judging by the sounds beneath the table so was the bone. It was only after he had ordered a second helping that Mr Moon began to look around the cafe. Although the journey had taken him twice as long as it should have, he did not imagine Mr O'Lovelife or the dwarf would have arrived before him. He guessed if they were tramping he would still be well ahead, and he was prepared to hang around the cafe for as long as necessary. But Mr Moon had not reckoned with the tramp's knowledge of the land and its many shortcuts, and so was thunderstruck when suddenly his eyes fell on a man who was obviously Mr O'Lovelife.

The tramp was alone. He was sitting on the far side of the room, in a corner against a window, and was idly drawing diagrams on the misted-up glass. Mr Moon waited, expecting the dwarf to appear, but when it became apparent this was not going to happen he approached the tramp.

'May I join you a moment?'

Mr O'Lovelife looked up to see a shabbily dressed old man standing beside him. He said nothing but indicated an empty chair across the table. Sitting down Mr Moon did not fail to notice the extra cup and plate on the table.

'I'm looking for someone,' he said.

'Then if it pleases you, carry on looking. I'm not one to interfere with another's business.'

'A friend of yours. The person you have been travelling with. It's imperative I find him.'

'I've been travelling with nobody,' snapped the tramp. 'I always travel alone. And what's it to you? I don't take much to strangers thrusting their company upon me.' With this he turned back to the window, ignoring Mr Moon.

The tramp's temper and secrecy surprised him. 'You could at least be a bit more civil,' he said.

'Civil? I've no intention of being civil. I gave it up long ago.'

'Perhaps,' said Mr Moon. 'But I imagine the person I'm trying to contact inspired in you something other than aggression. Curiosity perhaps?'

Mr O'Lovelife readjusted the crumpled carnation in his lapel. 'I'm curious about many things in this world,' said the tramp.

'And how about things from outside this world?' asked Mr Moon.

'Those too,' he said.

'I must find your friend,' pleaded Mr Moon. 'If you'll tell me where he's gone . . . ?'

'I can tell you nothing,' sniffed the tramp. 'My lips are sealed.'

And Mr O'Lovelife's lips were so tight they might as well

94

have been sealed. He felt any further conversation with the stranger would constitute a betrayal. Mr O'Lovelife was upset that the dwarf had deserted him, for he did not make friends easily, and usually he rejected the world before it found time to reject him. He pushed back his chair and gathering his case under his arm rose to go. But before he had a chance to move he was stopped by one of the lorry-drivers he had spoken to earlier.

'Did Paddy give your little friend a lift to Lewsbury, then?' he asked.

Before the tramp could deny it Mr Moon was hurrying out of the cafe. 'Lewsbury!' he cried. 'Lewsbury!' He ran between the lorries towards his motor car, Wanderlust splashing along behind him. The word Lewsbury echoed inside his head. Perhaps that was where he would find the dwarf.

18

AFTER so many rumours and so much speculation the schoolchildren had expected something more amazing than the ragged dwarf now hidden away beneath the coats at the back of the school-bus, and Nameon sensed their disappointment. He wished for their sakes he was a 'magic being', but he had never felt less magical in his entire life. At carnivals he had seen magicians change the colour of leaves and produce a hundred doves from a single cage, but it was all harmless trickery and he knew real magic was nothing to do with conjuring. He knew a great deal of magic was simply newness, and that things seen for the first time inevitably looked magical. Of course powerful magic did exist – it had brought him into the human world – but it was a very rare magic and hard for him to talk about. He did not know how to explain such things to the children. Like himself, they had been fed so many fantastic tales that the truth had become obscured. He was tired, and to speak of Oakwood made him feel homesick.

After a while the children grew sensitive enough to his moods to avoid pestering him. They realized it was by accident he had come into their world, and that he was anxious to return home. He seemed obsessed with a town called Norton Bay, and spoke of the place as if it were the centre of the universe. When asked why he wanted to go there in particular he muttered about maps and gates, and boats hidden away in forests. The children could make no sense of what he said. He sulked and shrugged his shoulders, as if the effort of explaining would exhaust him completely.

Not all the children were actively involved with SPLOT, nor were they all sympathetic towards the dwarf's plight. At the front of the bus a group of children sat laughing self-consciously and making rude remarks about bedtime and fairy-tales. Nameon tried to ignore them, but it was an effort to listen when the other children offered suggestions on how best he could get to Norton Bay. Ideas were put forward by the dozen: he could steal a horse and ride there, he could row up canals, he could go by balloon. Someone offered the loan of a bicycle and someone else offered him a pair of roller skates. The suggestions were highly imaginative, but utterly unrealistic. Being more down to earth, Benjamin Platts decided the quickest and safest way was of course by train. This seemed the perfect solution until it was discovered that Nameon had no 'real' money with which to purchase a ticket.

'We might be able to raise enough for the fare by tomorrow afternoon,' said Benjamin, 'but I've no idea how.'

'Then maybe I can help.'

The boy who had made the rather feeble joke about the statue in the cathedral swaggered down the gangway to the back of the bus. 'If you can cast a spell and change Mr Rabbitt into a frog, then I'll give you the money,' he announced.

There were yells of encouragement from the front seats.

'Real magic is nothing to do with –' Nameon stopped, suddenly aware that the boy was trying to make a fool of him. He retaliated quickly, for he thought ridicule a particularly nasty form of bullying. He stared the boy in the face. 'Go back to your friends,' he said, 'or I will change *you* into a frog. Dwarfs do not like to be offended, not even by human beings.'

Nameon glared at him. 'You have five seconds,' he said. 'I'll count the seconds backwards and if you are still here I'll cast the spell. You will leap out of the neck of your own shirt and hop back to your seat.'

The boy hesitated, but Nameon seemed so serious and confident that by the time the dwarf had counted down to four he had turned a bright pink and two seconds later was sitting back in his seat. His friends said nothing. They shuffled and pretended to be looking out of the window at Something Interesting.

Nameon's victory over the bully was complete, and he immediately rose in the children's estimation. They were convinced that had he wanted to, he would have had no trouble in carrying out his threat. Nameon thought it wise not to disillusion them.

Late in the afternoon the sun was lost behind a bank of clouds; it grew darker and the bus began to buzz with a new excitement. Benjamin Platts rearranged the pile of coats over Nameon. They were nearing Steelborough.

'Mr Rabbitt will be getting off the bus in a few minutes. Can you remember our plan?' he asked.

The coats nodded in reply.

'Are you sure?'

The coats nodded again.

'I'll repeat the instructions anyway. We've got to be methodical about things. Now, when Mr Rabbitt stops you get off the bus. We will direct you to an old bus shelter where you will wait for Johnny Plackham, who we will contact and tell to come and fetch you.' Benjamin looked at his watch. 'It might take a few hours for him to reach you, but it is the best we can do. It would be dangerous for you to come into the bus depot. We can deal with the problems of your train ticket tomorrow.

'We meet outside the Odeon at 2 p.m. sharp.'

'Outside the what?' asked Nameon, peering from beneath the coats.

'The Odeon,' said Benjamin, forgetting his official-type voice. 'It's a cinema, but there's no time to explain about it now. It will be packed with SPLOT people and safe enough.'

The school-bus slowed down. Mr Rabbitt pulled off the road into a brightly lit courtyard furnished with plastic seats, tables and, much to Nameon's disgust, plastic gnomes.

'I've got some business to attend to, so amuse yourselves for a few minutes,' he said, and climbing out of the bus he disappeared across the courtyard.

As soon as Mr Rabbitt was out of sight Nameon was led to the bus shelter. It was made of corrugated iron and contained a narrow wooden bench scarred by pen-knives and crude drawings. Set back from the road in a disused layby, it was a relic from the days before motorways existed, and was now seldom used.

When the children returned to the bus Nameon explored the shelter and finding the least draughty place sat down to examine the contents of a paper bag he had been given. It contained an orange, a half-eaten bar of chocolate, a piece of chewing-gum and a note that said, 'DON'T FORGET THE ODEON. 2 P.M. TOMORROW SIGNED SPLOT.' Half the chewing-gum he used to block a hole in his boot and the rest he swallowed.

An hour passed, and then another, and after a third hour Nameon began to wonder if Johnny Plackham would ever come. He had expected to wait longer than the children had said, knowing that even with the best-formed plans something inevitably went wrong, but after four hours he grew anxious and ventured out into the road.

On the same side of the road as the shelter was a steep bank covered in ferns and opposite was a hedge thick with dead leaves and quarrelsome sparrows. Wondering if the city could be seen from beyond the hedge Nameon crawled

99

through it and on the far side discovered a narrow strip of field falling abruptly into a valley. To his right on the valley's lowest slopes was a mass of lights, separated by pools of darkness. It was Steelborough, and to the dwarf it seemed as if a piece of the sky had fallen on to the hillside and shattered.

It grew steadily colder as time passed. He heard voices drifting from the public house several hundred yards away, and people laughed and crunched across the gravelled courtyard. Then doors slammed and motor cars growled into life.

And then there was only the darkness.

19

WHEN midnight struck in a tower across the valley Nameon began to think something had gone wrong and that the children had been unable to contact Johnny Plackham. He surveyed the road countless times, looking cautiously out of the shelter whenever the slightest sound caught his attention, but no one came.

That night he slept badly, and waking the following morning before dawn he decided to walk into the city alone.

The road was not much wider than a country lane and at that time of a winter morning was joyless. After half a mile or so the hedgerow ended and Nameon found himself on a high, open road. He sat down for a moment to readjust the paper in his boots, then he continued.

The countryside was a jumble of neglected fields and stubbly wasteland. Sheep grazed at the edge of the road and Nameon, clutching a large stick, hurried past them. The road dipped gently for several miles before disappearing behind a hill covered in moss and boulders. As Nameon walked the day grew lighter and the boulders caught the sun. For a moment they were like huge bloodstones set in the sides of the earth, but then gloom settled once more over the morning.

He began to pass farms set back from the road. Outside them were tractors and motor cars. He daydreamed about how nice it would be to be able to sit inside one and let it take him into Steelborough, but though he tried to remember how

Paddy had driven his lorry he doubted if he himself could manage to drive.

Then in a roadside ditch Nameon discovered a pram. He was not quite sure what it was, but as it had four wheels and a body he decided it must be a simpler version of a motor car. Nameon dragged it out of the ditch and climbed into it. Nothing happened. He climbed back out and was about to abandon the pram when it occurred to him that on a hill it would need no dials or engine. He pushed it until once more the road began to dip. And then he leapt back inside. He was delighted to find the pram still moved. The cold air refreshed him more than his brief sleep, and soon he felt exhilarated.

He was in a philosophic state of mind, musing over how good it was to be in another world, and so at first he did not notice when the pram began to gather speed. Soon he was averaging fourteen miles an hour. The fact that there was no brake to stop the pram moving had not occurred to him and, when it did, it did not bother him. He seemed to remember how in the distance the road curved and rose again, and thus the pram was bound to stop of its own accord. His scheme was to push the pram up hills and to ride down them.

On either side of him houses were becoming more numerous and the fields between them smaller. Individual sounds were lost in the day's inevitable noise. The smoother the road grew the more uncomfortable Nameon became, and when the pram finally reached the curve in the road he realized how little his sense of perspective was suited to a world not confined by oak trees. Rather than rise again as he had expected, the road plunged giddily. He was on the outskirts of Steelborough, and below him the city lay engulfed in fumes and built predominantly of stone.

There seemed to be no way of stopping the pram. On either side of the road were factories fronted by wire fences and huge gates. People came to the edge of the pavement and stood staring as the bewildered dwarf sped past. Some waved and some shouted, and others turned pale. The speed of the pram increased from fourteen miles an hour to over twenty, and the wheels began to wobble. He was terrified. He felt sick and wanted to scream but with the wind as well as his heart in his mouth he couldn't.

Soon he was entering a more crowded part of the city. People muffled against the cold rushed after him but were left behind, winded and helpless. The wheels wobbled dangerously and the pram changed course. It crashed up on to a pavement, spun round and, miraculously still upright, continued its journey minus a wheel.

After what seemed a century it skidded into a small side street, one of many that led off the main road and here at last it came to a halt. Nameon crawled out dazed, dizzy and more than a little sick. He was bruised, but the thickness of his coat and his pockets stuffed with apples had saved him from more drastic injury. Somewhere behind him he heard the muted sound of a siren and humans shouting.

He came to his senses fast enough to realize the noise had something to do with his pram journey, and he quickly put as much distance between the pram and himself as possible. The streets zigzagged across each other, leading always to identical-looking streets. At least they would have seemed identical had not all the doors been painted different colours. The bright reds and greens of the painted wood contrasted oddly with the sense of dereliction that hung over the neighbourhood. On the corners of most streets were either shabby public houses or shops with windows that seemed to be advertising dust. In this maze Nameon was lost. Some houses were boarded up and across walls were scrawled messages he did not understand. There were faded posters of women holding tins, and pictures of children walking up long avenues hand in hand.

Then a small notice caught his attention. It was on the wall of a semi-derelict street that faced a shop doorway in which he was standing regaining his breath. The sign read: Micawber Street, S'bourgh 7.

At first Nameon could not think why that particular street-sign stood out from the rest, but then he remembered having been told Johnny Plackham's address. It was the same street, but try as he might he could not remember the number of the house.

There were seventy houses in the street, and at least a third of these were derelict.

Nameon wandered aimlessly up and down the pavement. On some doors were bells with names printed neatly beside them, but most doors gave no indication as to who lived behind them. He reached the end of the street and was about to cross the road and walk back down it for the umpteenth time when a man ambled into sight carrying a large sack over his shoulder. The man stopped almost opposite Nameon and taking from the sack a wad of paper proceeded to push it through a hole in one of the doors. He glanced at Nameon without much interest, and then disappeared back round the street corner.

One piece of paper still hung out of the door. Intrigued as to what the man had been up to Nameon crossed the road and pulled it out. It was a letter addressed to Johnny Plackham, Secretary of SPLOT.

20

JOHNNY PLACKHAM sat spying through the parlour window. He was dressed in grubby pyjamas and his eyes were thick with sleep. It was the first morning he had risen before eleven for weeks, except for one occasion when he had begrudgingly put in an appearance at school. There was a reason for Johnny's early rising. The previous evening the house had been besieged by a group of idiotic children who had informed him rather breathlessly of how they'd found a leprechaun in Lewsbury Cathedral and brought it to the outskirts of Steelborough, leaving it in a disused bus shelter.

It sounded highly improbable to Johnny. He thought it might be a hoax, but decided to take no chances. Everywhere he had been recently he'd had to play-act, talking seriously about SPLOT's role in keeping its hero out of the hands of grown-ups. He had never for a moment actually believed the creature existed, but it suited his purpose to pretend he did.

After the delegation had delivered its message and been curtly dismissed, Johnny did some hard thinking and came to the conclusion that they were in fact sincere. But even if the leprechaun did exist and was stranded on the outskirts of the city, Johnny Plackham had no intentions of tramping out into a wet January night to retrieve the creature.

If he had been tall, Johnny Plackham would have been the perfect bully. But he was small and ratty. At school he was considered lazy and unintelligent, but his teachers were wrong. His intelligence was of a kind more suited to the streets and crumbled houses among which he lived than to geometry and arithmetic. He was adept at taking money out of gas meters and at emptying ten pence pieces from telephone booths. He was also adept at not being caught. Some of his friends ended up in police stations, but never Johnny. He was as cunning a piece of work as ever swopped short trousers for long ones.

His father, Mr Plackham, said that anyone who could get his name into the newspapers could make money, and he firmly believed that all those who appeared on television became millionaires overnight. Mr Plackham had never had his name in the newspapers and had never appeared on television, but still Johnny believed him, which was surprising, as usually he believed very little Mr Plackham said. When his chance came to appear on television Johnny had jumped at the opportunity, though then he'd no notion how he could turn his sudden and brief fame to his financial advantage.

It did not take long to discover a method. After dismissing various possible schemes as too fanciful he hit on the idea of a subscription fund. For the sum of fifty pence anyone could become a member of SPLOT, all payments to be made, of course, to the Secretary and Treasurer, Johnny Plackham. A couple more appearances on television as Secretary of the Society and a mention or two in the newspapers had been all the advertisement he had needed.

When the letters started pouring into 29 Micawber Street three-quarters of them contained postal orders for fifty pence and requests for SPLOT membership. At first he laboriously made and sent hand-written membership certificates, but eventually he simply ignored the letters and collected the money.

Of course Mr Plackham knew something was up, but whenever he was about to tackle Johnny, Johnny came home with gifts of cigarettes and whiskey and little things that made life easier. Mrs Plackham said nothing, either. A milk-bill paid and groceries bought lightened a burden, and anyway neither believed that Johnny would do anything *really* criminal.

Only his younger brother thought Johnny was a criminal. But Tobias Plackham did not count.

On the night of his strange visit Johnny had gone to bed in an evil temper. The last thing he wanted was to look after a leprechaun. But then during the night a new scheme formed in his shrewd and quite possibly twisted brain. He sat up, cursing himself for not thinking of it immediately.

The flow of postal orders had diminished, and Johnny reckoned it would be only a matter of weeks before they stopped arriving altogether. The way things were going he could expect only another five or ten pounds before both the gullibility and enthusiasm for SPLOT fizzled out. But, he wondered, how much would he be able to make if he actually trapped the leprechaun?

Now, through a gap in the curtains, Johnny watched the leprechaun as a spider might watch a large and juicy fly. He had been watching for a long time and for a long time the creature had been walking indecisively up and down the street. 'Creature' was perhaps the wrong word for the leprechaun did not look quite how Johnny had imagined. In his mind's eye had always been a vague picture, based on illustrations in books he had long outgrown. He had imagined a creature no larger than a monkey, a creature with gossamer wings and extremely pointed ears, certainly not one wearing enormous hobnailed boots and a raggy coat. Johnny was also quick to notice that beneath the absurd clothes the leprechaun looked by no means weak or effeminate. He doubted if he could overcome it by physical force, as had been his original intention.

He thought of enlisting the help of his father who was still snoring in the room above him, but realized the appearance of Mr Plackham would have an undesirable effect on the creature. Next he thought of enlisting the help of Tobias, but knew Tobias would be unlikely to fall in with his plans. He finally decided on a scheme that seemed foolproof. It was anyway the only one that occurred to him so early in the morning when his brain was still half-asleep.

He had been musing over his plan when the postman passed the window and he heard the now familiar flop of letters on to the floor. Looking out at an angle he saw the postman had caught the leprechaun's attention and that it was dithering on the far side of the road, not knowing quite what to do. Then the creature crossed the road.

Johnny let the curtain fall back. He heard a shuffling on the pavement and then a letter that had remained jammed in the letterbox vanished.

21

WHEN Johnny Plackham opened the door suddenly, Nameon froze. He had never seen such a disagreeable-looking face. His first instinct was to turn and run, but something held him back. The thought, 'But this is Johnny Plackham,' rushed meaninglessly through his mind.

'Shh,' said the boy, 'Shh.' And then, 'You'd better come inside before anyone sees you.'

Remembering the pram and the attention it had attracted Nameon stepped into the house, where he was immediately relieved of the letter he had been clutching.

The room smelt of furniture polish. Everything shone and looked unused. A new bicycle rested against a piano piled high with comics and to one of the walls clung three chalk ducks, one above the other, as if frozen in their attempts to escape from the room.

'Now there's a coincidence,' lied Johnny Plackham, 'I was just this very moment coming out to collect you.'

'Oh?'

'Yes, I was just coming to the bus shelter. I had homework to do last night. Didn't anyone come and tell you?'

'No one appeared last night,' said the dwarf.

'It goes to show how unreliable people are, doesn't it?'

The boy seemed ill at ease and fidgety. 'Why don't you take off your coat?' he asked. 'You must be exhausted.' Nameon struggled out of his coat and Johnny hung it on a painted nail behind the front door. 'That's better,' he said. 'You look more like yourself now. Are you very small without those boots? I bet they're uncomfortable.' Nameon said that he would rather leave his boots on.

While his dubious host was in the kitchen making coffee Nameon instinctively took his overcoat off the nail and sat down again with it resting across his knees. He felt he might have to leave in a hurry, but was reluctant to move. Johnny Plackham came back with a cup of coffee which he offered to Nameon. It was bitter, and the dwarf would have preferred water.

'I don't want to be funny,' said the boy, taking the neglected coffee for himself, 'I believe you are what you are, but many wouldn't. Now if you had something unusual with which we could persuade them?'

'Persuade who?' asked Nameon. 'Surely the last thing we want is for people to know what I am. They might –'

'Persuade the kids,' said Johnny. 'Persuade the kids to help us.'

'But they have already,' said Nameon. 'They don't need persuasion.'

But Johnny was adamant about what he called evidence, and so Nameon reluctantly gave him one of his four remaining coins. 'It's an Acorn-and-Hollyhock,' he said. 'What you would call fairy-money.'

There followed an awkward silence during which Nameon fidgeted with his coat and Johnny fidgeted with the coffee-cup. Then under the pretext that his father would soon be getting up, Johnny suggested that Nameon wait out in the backyard while he went and arranged things.

'What kind of things?' asked Nameon.

'Things to help. You don't seem to trust me much, do you?'

He led Nameon through the kitchen, a tiny room littered with cups and newspapers, into the backyard. Running

down one wall of the yard was a narrow stretch of earth too small to be termed a garden, and against it hung a shrivelled creeper. Farther down was a shed, against which was piled a mass of junk.

'Down here,' said Johnny. 'It's much safer down here.'

Nameon looked at the shed. 'I think it would be better if I just left,' he said.

'Left? But I've spent days preparing this shed for your comfort. Days! It would be terrible if you deserted me now. Can you imagine what the Society would think? They would say I'd mistreated you. You don't understand the responsibilities I have. In fact, I'm beginning to think you are ungrateful.'

'I'm certainly not ungrateful, but –'

'And after bringing you all the way from Lewsbury. Lewsbury of all places! You'd have been caught there for certain.'

'That was very kind, but –'

'Just come down and take a look.'

'I'll take a look, then I really must leave,' said Nameon, his heart sinking at the thought that perhaps he was about to be betrayed.

22

TOBIAS PLACKHAM was woken by the sound of a scuffle and the slamming of a shed door. He knelt up on his bed and wiping condensation from the window looked down into the yard. His brother was hurrying up to the kitchen limping slightly, as if he'd received a kick on the shin.

Recently the brothers had not been on the best of terms, or rather had been on even worse terms than usual. While not actually proud that his elder brother was the secretary, treasurer, and self-styled president of SPLOT, Tobias himself was committed to the Society, of which he was the first honorary member (a position Johnny had given him gratis in the hope that he would keep quiet about the postal orders). Tobias had kept quiet, but for a reason that Johnny did not suspect. He was ashamed of his brother. He dressed quickly and sensing something was amiss hurried down the stairs.

23

MR Moon arrived in Lewsbury a few hours after Paddy dropped Nameon off. He immediately found a decently priced hotel as a base from which to search for the dwarf, and by nine o'clock in the morning had washed and, for the first time in weeks, shaved. By 9.30, still exhausted from his drive but temporarily refreshed, he was in the market-place asking questions. But by then most of the lorry-drivers were gone, and nobody knew of a man called Paddy. By 10.30 the effects of his wash and brush up had worn off, and by 11 a.m. he was aimlessly following any small person who remotely resembled his image of Nameon.

In a supermarket at 11.30 he caused acute embarrassment to himself and a 'goblin' whom he grabbed by the shoulders after crashing through a horde of shoppers. The goblin turned out to be a child in a mask.

At noon he was again wandering aimlessly through the market, which had now changed appearance and was lined with stalls selling trinkets, pots and clothes. Never once did he think of searching the parks.

At 12.30 Mr Moon found himself outside the archaeological museum in the cathedral close. He was going to bypass the museum but saw Wanderlust lingering at the entrance. He decided to take a look inside. The museum contained only objects of local origin and was attended by a rotund gentleman in a blue uniform who was dozing at a desk in the corner and did not notice them enter.

There were several cases containing rusty knives and what might or might not have been arrow-heads; there were Roman coins, bracelets, rings and a few cases of odd-looking bones. Mr Moon soon grew impatient. He walked towards the door expecting Wanderlust to join him, but the dog refused to move and stayed grinning and wagging its tail at the foot of the still sleeping attendant.

Mr Moon had coffee and sandwiches in a cafe crowded with infants and harassed mothers, then at 1.30 in a stationer's shop he bought a map of the city and the surrounding area. He studied it, then threw it away. The city was small, but still too large for the map to be of any use to him. The dwarf could be anywhere. Near, far, anywhere. He wandered the crowded streets and the more he searched the more miserable Mr Moon became.

He sat down on a street bench exhausted and close to tears. He was frustrated at having followed his quarry for so long, only to totally lose it. He watched a school-bus pull out from the cathedral close and disappear into the traffic. Suddenly the world seemed too crowded for Mr Moon. He felt defeated. At five o'clock in the evening, hardly able to keep his eyes open and believing his search for Nameon well and truly over, he returned to the hotel and collapsed fully dressed on to his bed.

Mr Moon slept solidly through the night and the following morning, waking only when the chambermaid tapped irritably at his bedroom door, complaining that it was late and that she wanted to tidy the room. 'I'll be out in half an hour,' he called and, shuffling over to the basin, splashed water on to his face. The basin gurgled and emptied itself. He pulled back the curtains and looked out at the dreary afternoon.

It was raining again. The water gushed down unseen

drains and to Mr Moon's ears it seemed the rain was laughing. It came accompanied by rolling thunder and occasional distant flashes of lightning. Mr Moon felt that there was something ominous about the rain. It penetrated his moods and seemed to isolate him from everything but his obsessions. It made the world look sad and grey, and everything in it seemed lost. He thought it a dismal day to return to Brumble Head and fall back into habits that no longer had any relevance to his life.

Into his case he threw a few grubby shirts, a towel, and a pair of creased trousers. On top of them he threw his book, which he no longer felt inclined to read. It was far too late to have breakfast at the hotel, and as it did not cater for lunches he paid his bill and left. He dumped his case into his car and hurried to the nearby railway station.

For an hour or more he sat in the station buffet, eating cheese sandwiches and idly watching people out on the platform. They were all waiting impatiently for trains that had no intention of arriving before they were due. He wanted to move, but there was nowhere he really wanted to go. Someone had left the door of the cafeteria ajar and when he stood to close it Mr Moon noticed through the windows a commotion at the far end of the platform. Much to his surprise he saw the attendant from the museum he had visited the previous day. The man was shouting and waving his arms and around him were grouped a porter, a passenger, a child, and a very thin policeman. They seemed concerned with what the attendant was saying. When he had finished gesticulating the group moved along the platform towards the buffet. Just as they did so and just as Mr Moon, disinterested, was about to close the door, in rushed a muddy and exhausted Wanderlust.

The dog scrambled under the table behind Mr Moon's and released from its jaws a huge bone. Attached to one end of it was a neatly printed tag that bore the inscription '*c.* 50 AD'. Fumbling under the table Mr Moon attempted to retrieve the bone. Although he managed to grab one end of it the dog clung resolutely to the other until, hearing voices outside, it growled what might have been a sigh of defeat and reluctantly let go. Mr Moon quickly sat down at his own table and, placing the bone on his plate, covered it with the remainder of his sandwiches and his hat. The door flew open and in marched the attendant followed by the policeman.

'We're looking for a bone, a valuable bone,' he wheezed.

'Well, to be more precise, sir,' said the policeman, 'we're looking for the dog that stole the bone.'

'The dog is not as important as the bone,' said the attendant irritably. 'We are looking for the bone.'

'And we've a fair description of the animal,' continued the policeman. 'It appears the creature is a small to middling mongrel with dark, unruly fur.'

'It smelt,' said the attendant.

Under the table Wanderlust snorted.

'Pardon?'

'I sniffed,' said Mr Moon, sniffing. 'If I see either the dog or the bone I will inform you at once. Now, if you don't mind, either come in or go out, but shut the door. It's rather cold.'

The company turned and hurried back outside.

Mr Moon quickly hid the bone but Wanderlust was a more substantial problem.

He finished his tea, but refrained from touching the ham sandwiches, which now had an unsavoury smell about them. On a table near him was a folded newspaper. He took the paper, and coaxing Wanderlust out from under the table wrapped it round the uncooperative mongrel. The dog wriggled furiously, not knowing what was best for it, but Mr Moon clung tightly and walked towards the exit. The railway porter, the museum attendant and the policeman, were now on the opposite platform. The attendant was gesticulating and still convinced the dog was somewhere close at hand. Mr Moon walked quickly into the road, not letting the dog go until he reached the motor car. He shoved Wanderlust inside, where the hard-done-by creature gave another indignant snort and settled more comfortably into its seat. It slept, dreaming about the glorious bone that had been so rudely taken from it.

Mr Moon sat behind the wheel and uncrumpled the newspaper. It was the afternoon edition of the *National Evening News*. He folded it carefully and was about to leave it in the glove compartment to read later when an astonishing headline caught his attention. It said:

LEPRECHAUN FOUND IN STEELBOROUGH
HOAX OR FACT?

Mr Moon looked across the road at the station clock. It was 4.30. The edition of the newspaper he held had been printed less than two hours ago.

The trail had not been lost.

24

TOBIAS PLACKHAM found his brother in the kitchen. He was industriously opening envelopes, taking out postal orders and discarding the letters attached to them. Tobias was familiar with this process, only it usually happened in the afternoon, and his brother's early rising bothered him.

Ignoring Johnny, he made himself a cup of coffee and stood staring out the kitchen window. He thought what a drab morning it was, but then remembering it was Saturday he brightened up. Saturday he loved best. Saturday was the one day he was left totally to his own devices. And the best thing about Saturday was going to the cinema in the afternoon.

'How do you spell advantageous?' asked Johnny.

'What?'

'Advantageous. You're the speller in the family.'

'What do you want to spell advantageous for?'

'A letter. What do you think?'

'You mean you are actually answering one of those letters?' asked Tobias.

'So what?'

'So it's unusual. What's the sentence?'

'It would be advantageous to your circulation.'

'That's a funny thing to put in a letter.'

Tobias, still looking out of the window, spelt 'advantageous'. 'It's a letter to a newspaper or something, isn't it?'

'Mind your own business.'

'I bet you're trying to sell them something.' Tobias finished his coffee and buttered some toast that had been left under the grill the previous evening. He let Johnny struggle on with his letter for a few minutes, and then said, 'It's Sunday tomorrow.'

'So what?'

'There's no post.'

This had not occurred to Johnny. He had planned on keeping the dwarf locked in the shed for a day or two while newspapers bid for an exclusive photograph and interview, after which he hoped to sell Nameon to a private zoo. But on reconsideration his latest scheme was full of flaws. Johnny wondered how long it would have taken him to break out of the shed if he were in the dwarf's position and realized it would take only a matter of hours with applied effort.

He crumpled up his letter, and throwing it on a pile searched through a stack of newspapers that had been tidied away under a chair cushion. He found a copy of the *National Evening News*.

The *National Evening News* boasted the largest circulation of any evening newspaper. It carried stories of how grandmothers had rescued budgies from the mouths of cats and printed large photographs of beauty queens who never looked beautiful. Its Steelborough office was on the far side of town, under a railway bridge where the street was perpetually damp and the air perpetually gloomy. In small type at the bottom of the sports page was printed the address and telephone number of the local office.

'I'm going out to make a phone call. Don't go out into the yard. Dad says he doesn't want his pigeons disturbed this morning – he's going to fly them.' Johnny put on a coat over his pyjamas and searched the mantelpiece for change.

'You've got good ears.'

'What do you mean?'

'Saying Dad says he doesn't want his pigeons disturbed. Did he shout that out in his sleep?'

'You're too clever,' said Johnny.

Tobias continued to stare out of the window. 'They sound more disturbed than usual, anyway,' he commented.

'Then don't disturb them more than they are. I'll only be gone for a few minutes.'

'You'll be gone longer than that,' said Tobias, staring intently at the pigeon shed. 'The phone-box down the road's out of order. You'll have to go to the one in Ashfield Street.'

Johnny muttered something unrepeatable, then went out.

Nameon was sitting on a stack of potatoes in the shed lamenting his stupidity. On the shelves above him the pigeons flapped about. He tried putting his shoulder to the door but he merely managed to bruise his arm. The shed was dark, its only light coming from a small window above him. He sat on the potatoes wondering how long it would be before something even more awful happened. He felt sick at the thought of having let himself be caught so easily. Oakwood had never seemed so far away.

He was brooding about Oakwood when he heard somebody rummaging outside. He crouched, ready to leap at whoever opened the door. In his hand he held a length of lead piping and he didn't care who was outside. But the door remained closed, and the rummaging and clinking continued.

Outside the shed Tobias Plackham was piling up cans and broken chairs in order to reach the tiny window.

'Hey,' he whispered, 'is anyone there?'

Nameon straightened up. It was not Johnny's voice. It was a gentler, more timid voice. A small, bright face peered through the window.

'You're the goblin, aren't you?' it inquired.

Nameon grunted, thinking that perhaps he was already on show.

'We're not all like my brother, he's just – he's awful.' Tobias Plackham wanted to apologize for what Johnny had done, but he didn't know how. 'I think he's gone to phone the newspapers and try to sell you. Here.'

Tobias pushed a small hacksaw through the window. 'This is all I can find. You'll have to try and saw through a plank. Johnny's taken the shed keys.'

Nameon scrambled across the potatoes and retrieved the saw from where it had fallen.

'We've not much time,' Tobias said. 'I'll keep guard. I'm quite good at keeping guard.'

The hacksaw had seen better days. It had also seen better years. It had seen them while hanging from a nail in the yard. It was frail and rusty, and its teeth were blunt. It took Nameon ten minutes to get the saw's teeth firmly established in the wood. Then slowly and laboriously he began to saw. Tobias stayed clinging to the window, able to see nothing inside the shed, but constantly complaining about his brother's bad character.

Johnny Plackham had believed his brother's statement about the telephone-box in the next street being out of order. It often was, and it was usually Johnny who damaged it. When he reached Ashfield Street he discovered that that kiosk was also out of order. In another five minutes he had found one near the gasworks.

When the leprechaun story first attracted attention Johnny had been interviewed by a copious young man of about twenty called William D'Arcy. When the journalist listened to him as one might listen to a young child telling amusing lies he had felt insulted, but it was an insult he had had to bear. He'd blabbed on about the Society for the Prevention of Cruelty to Leprechauns and the journalist had nodded wisely and taken notes. When leaving, the journalist had said, 'If you get any more news let me know, especially if you discover where the leprechaun is.'

And so now Johnny Plackham was letting him know.

He dialled the number he wanted and inserted his money in the pay-box.

'Hello?'

'I want to speak to William D'Arcy.'

'Who's calling, please?'

'It's personal.'

There was a pause and then another voice.

'D'Arcy speaking.'

'This is Johnny Plackham.'

'Who?'

'Johnny Plackham.'

'I'm afraid I can't –'

'The President of the Leprechaun Society.'

'Oh, yes?' William D'Arcy didn't sound interested. He had not liked Johnny.

'You remember saying that you'd be interested in any further information about the leprechaun?'

'It seems such a long time ago,' said the journalist.

'If you're not interested, I could always tell the *Steelborough Times*,' said Johnny, sensing the journalist's indifference.

The *Steelborough Times* was only a local paper, but as local papers sometimes sell stories to larger papers, D'Arcy knew he'd be a fool if there was anything newsworthy he ignored. 'What's your information?' he asked.

'Will you pay for it?'

'It depends on whether or not we use the story.'

Johnny hesitated and then, 'The leprechaun's actually been found. It's an exclusive for you.'

'Yes?'

'Yes. It's here in Steelborough. I've got it locked in the pigeon shed and it's genuine.'

William D'Arcy said he would call round to the house and Johnny put down the telephone. He stood tapping his fingers on the pay-box. The journalist had not been very forthcoming about money. Johnny flipped through the phone book.

He phoned the *Steelborough Times*, the *News'* rival. He phoned two television stations, the zoo, the RSPCA, a couple of local radio stations, and several local photography agencies. To do this he broke open the pay-box on which his fingers had been drumming. And then Johnny went home to await the result of his labours. 'I'll auction the stupid thing to the highest bidder,' he thought.

When Johnny came into view Tobias was sitting on the doorstep watching the street, and Nameon was still in the pigeon shed working furiously with the blunt and now broken saw. Tobias locked the front door and rushed through the house into the yard. As he reached the shed there was a loud crack and a hobnailed boot burst through the planks. Nameon squeezed through the gap and together they fled out the back door into an alleyway smelling of garbage and littered with bricks and cans.

Tobias weaved his way through the alleys. He knew them better than the streets which they occasionally crossed. Nameon mistook them for poorer versions of the streets and expected to find a different kind of human being living in them, but the only person he saw was an old lady who carried on her back a sackful of clinking bottles. She wore a black coat buttoned tightly, and on her head a green and yellow scarf. She made a living by foraging among the rubbish the rest of the world had discarded, and was nearly as small as himself.

When Tobias led Nameon out of the alleys and into the streets they were in a different part of the city. The roads were wider and instead of small dusty shops there were large stores, similar to those he had seen in Lewsbury. A few hundred yards from the alley's entrance was a cinema and outside it stood a line of children.

The cinema was the main event in Tobias Plackham's otherwise ordinary week, and he was delighted to be able to share it with Nameon. He had enough money to buy two tickets and one ice-cream, and he could think of no better hiding place for the dwarf, and certainly no better way of showing Nameon his world. Standing in the queue he enthused about the serial he had been following for the last eleven weeks. Nameon, several inches smaller than most of the crowd, stood listening but unable to comprehend what Tobias was talking about. A murmur of recognition passed along the queue. Nameon had been expected.

'You're going to love the cinema,' said Tobias.

25

THE manager of the Odeon watched the children entering the cinema. There was a larger crowd than usual and they seemed unnaturally excited. It was the one day of the week Mr Fisher wished he had a different kind of job. Today, however, the children were whispering loudly instead of shouting, and although he knew he should be thankful for such an odd occurrence, it made him feel uneasy. He would have preferred the pushing, the hat-snatching and the wailing. He would have known where he was then. For a moment he thought he had made a terrible blunder, like Mr Wallace, the manager of the Magnet, who had once accidentally chosen a violent horror film to show the children. Mr Fisher hurried along to the projectionist's box, checked the reels of film, and found nothing amiss. He questioned Miss Fuller and Miss Smith, the usherettes, and Mr Kemp the projectionist, but though all agreed the cinema was unusually crowded and the crowd unusually excited, no one could offer an explanation.

When he returned to the foyer the last of the children were disappearing into the auditorium and already the marble floor was littered with sweet-papers and orange peel. Mr Fisher stood on the cinema steps, breathing in the cold air, filling and emptying his lungs as if exercising prior to an endurance test.

In the traffic outside he noticed within five minutes two

different television crews, several radio trucks and William D'Arcy, a journalist friend of his, all heading in the same direction. An RSPCA van was having engine trouble opposite the traffic lights, and somewhere a fire-engine was wailing continually. People were turning their heads, shrugging, and pointing vaguely towards the gasworks.

Inside, the film show started with the usual booing and stamping of feet that accompanied the adverts and that proved to Mr Fisher the children knew nothing about the economics of the cinema. The stamping was followed by murmurs of approval and disapproval, indicating that the trailers for the following Saturday were already showing. It was at this point that Mr Fisher usually left the steps and entered the dark and overheated auditorium. He always insisted on the projectionist showing the cartoon after the trailers. This week it was a cartoon called *Kindness to Mice Week* and both he and the children enjoyed it.

Nameon was sitting somewhere in the centre of the crowd next to Tobias and flanked by Benjamin Platts who had met them in the foyer. The size of the screen and the luxuriant colour put Mrs Butler's crystal in the shade.

Nameon was oblivious of his companions. They plotted and whispered in low voices. Tobias related the whole sordid story of his brother's betrayal and the children agreed to denounce him as soon as possible, but insisted the major issue was to get Nameon safely to Norton Bay. Samuel Oken, a SPLOT lieutenant, had been dispatched to the station to gather information and timetables and returned just before the serial began.

'There's nowt till the one-thirty tonight,' he said, 'and a one-way ticket costs –' he looked at the paper on which he'd written the details, '£14.75.'

'But he's not got that kind of money, surely?' asked Tobias.

'No, he's only got fairy-money.'

'That sounds even better,' said Tobias.

'That's not the point. It's worthless here.'

'It's very much the point,' Tobias continued, 'I was wondering what Johnny would do if he was on our side. He'd get the real money easily.'

'How?'

'He'd raffle off the fairy-money, of course. He'd hold a lottery.'

'Marvellous,' said Benjamin. 'We'll tear paper into tickets and everyone who wants to join in can write their name on a piece. We'll charge ten pence a ticket, put all the tickets in a hat, shuffle them, and the name we pull out will get the dwarf's coins.'

'We'll do it after the main film,' said Tobias.

'No, we'll do it in the interval,' said Benjamin.

It was decided, and the message was passed around.

When Tobias turned his attention back to Nameon he found the dwarf had not been listening to the conversation at all. He was totally engrossed in the serial that had just begun.

The serial was called *Cosmo-Man*, and involved an astronaut who, while on a mission to a space-station, had crashed through a time-warp and been stranded in another universe. His only hope of returning home was to relocate the time-warp. This week Cosmo-Man had eventually found it again and was preparing to fly back into his own universe when winged lizards suddenly appeared. Cosmo-Man was in a dilemma: the time-warp only materialized briefly before vanishing to appear elsewhere, probably light years away. The astronaut could either pass back into his own universe and chance the lizards not following him; or he could stay and fight, letting the time-warp close against him. Nameon thought that in many ways the astronaut's predicament was similar to his own, and when Cosmo-Man turned back and valiantly faced the on-coming lizards, Nameon felt humbled.

He doubted if he would be able to summon up the same kind of courage, and fell to wondering if any similar creatures existed in Norton Bay.

Nameon was never to find out whether or not the astronaut overcame the lizards, for at the height of the battle the accompanying music swelled, the film blurred, and a loud voice informed the children that if they wished to know the outcome of the battle they would have to return the following week.

Infuriated by the sudden disappearance of Cosmo-Man, Nameon stood up on his folded seat and shouted that he wouldn't be in the cinema next week and wanted to know what happened immediately. He was pulled down by Tobias and Benjamin. He was highly involved with Cosmo-Man's dilemma and it took several of the children to convince him that such abrupt endings were usual, otherwise the serial wouldn't be a serial. 'Anyway, Cosmo-Man is bound to win, he can't *really* lose,' said Tobias.

'Nonsense,' said Nameon, still annoyed, 'the lizards looked ferocious.'

Benjamin sighed. 'The lizards are not real,' he said.

The lights were now on in the auditorium and Miss Fuller and Miss Smith were standing in the aisles with trays of ice-cream. Mr Fisher distinctly heard the tinkle of coins mixed in with the chatter of voices, but when only twenty-five per cent of the children who usually bought ices rose from their seats, he was both puzzled and cross. He was cross because the sale of ice-creams, specially on Saturday after-noons, represented an important part of his profit. He felt it a personal insult when the children refused to part with their money. He was puzzled because, with the cinema crowded, he had expected to sell more ice-creams than usual.

In his office, decorated with faded photographs of faded

filmstars, Mr Fisher telephoned Mr Wallace, his rival at the Magnet cinema. He wanted to know if Mr Wallace was experiencing any similar goings-on.

There followed a strained phone conversation during which Mr Wallace informed Mr Fisher that the Magnet cinema was almost empty and that he, Mr Fisher, was entirely to blame.

'You've been spreading rumours to gullible children,' he said.

'Why on earth should I spread rumours?' asked the puzzled Mr Fisher.

Mr Wallace did not answer his question. He spluttered and rambled on about leprechauns hiding in cinemas, and grew more and more agitated. Mr Fisher put down the telephone, his ears burning with abuse.

In the auditorium the clinking of the coins continued and soon two caps were filled with money and several more with slips of paper on which those who had paid to enter the lottery had written their names. The caps were returned to the centre rows where Tobias and Benjamin Platts counted the money. There was enough for the train ticket. The main feature was about to begin.

The lottery had been explained to Nameon during the interval and the time of the train he must catch written out on a scrap of paper. 'All you've got to do is pick a name from the hat and we'll announce the winner,' Tobias said.

Nameon looked at the delighted faces around him and was moved by how much the children wanted to help. Even the older children. Falling in with the enthusiasm of their younger friends they bought tickets, not wanting to show the reservations they felt about the dwarf. Some thought him nothing more than a small confidence trickster preying on the credulity of juniors, while others decided he was a harmless lunatic who had actually deluded himself into believing he was from another world. But these thoughts they were prepared to keep to themselves.

Nameon took out the remaining coins. He thought the children's wish to believe in another world more magical than the coins themselves, and suddenly he wanted to give them concrete evidence that another world did exist.

'I'll announce the winner myself,' he said, leaving his seat.

The feature film was one of a string of dull cowboy movies that had been hired cheaply and which the children often found boring. They hissed and booed at the various characters not because they cared, but because hissing and booing made the afternoon more exciting and relieved the monotony of the all-too-familiar stories. That their imaginations were larger and less easily satisfied than his own was something Mr Fisher had never considered.

In the front of the auditorium Nameon discovered a small door. Opening it he found himself in a passageway that led directly behind the screen, and off this passage were a number of changing rooms used whenever the cinema was transformed back into a theatre. In one of the changing rooms he took off his overcoat and boots, leaving himself dressed only in the dragon-skin vest and ragged, ill-fitting trousers. In a cupboard he found a theatrical make-up box and kneeling on a chair in front of a mirror lit by miniature bulbs he applied the make-up. He distorted the natural slant of his eyes, and exaggerated the shape of his mouth, and then from a table he took a pair of long scissors. A final glance and he was satisfied that, at last, he looked how the world expected him to be. He moved back along the passageway behind the canvas and, deafened by the sound of gunshots and galloping hooves, with the scissors he bravely slashed through the screen.

Crawling through the canvas out on to a narrowish platform, Nameon's vest was immediately caught in the

projectionist's beam. Above the sound of the celluloid voices he called out his own name, which to him sounded unnecessarily dramatic. Behind him on the torn screen the images continued to flicker, only now they were lit with the additional, unfamiliar colours his vest reflected. Dragon skin is like shot silk and when it catches the light it glows and can be mistaken for flames.

The projectionist, like the children, was mesmerized by the apparition and in his confusion speeded up the film.

After shouting out his name in such a dramatic fashion, Nameon knew it would be an anticlimax simply to announce the winner of the lottery. So, shy as he was under ordinary circumstances, he began an extraordinary dance.

His dancing was unlike any human dance. It was one he had witnessed at festivals and carnivals in his own world, one he had never learnt but knew how to imitate. It was a dragon dance, and though time had dimmed his memory he now moved through the rituals of the dancers he had seen when he himself had been a child. He spun round slowly, letting the scales on the skin glow and merge into each other. The children, the projectionist, Mr Fisher, Miss Fuller and Miss Smith were too astounded to move. They saw a mass of burning yet gentle colour, over which the speeded film played, and through which floated a grotesque dwarf, booming out its name. It was real magic: one moment on the screen was something which barely held the attention, and the next instant was something to which the imagination clung and refused to let go.

Billy Owen, the obnoxious youth who had taunted Nameon on the school-bus and whom Nameon had threatened to turn into a frog, opened his mouth in amazement and out fell several large gob-stoppers. They rolled under the seats and remained unclaimed.

With his dancing Nameon hypnotized the entire cinema.

The children felt sleepy, then were no longer in Steelborough but in Oakwood, surrounded by gremlins, dragons and carnival dwarfs. They smelt the scent of bark burning on open fires and of the winter flowers that grew at the forest's edge, and the scents and images were not vague but sharp and real. For Nameon it was a mixture of play-acting, make-up and make-believe, but he dearly wanted his illusion to work. Only Tobias escaped being mesmerized. He was too preoccupied with thinking about his brother, and kept craning his neck round to see if Johnny had guessed where they were hiding. And, of course, Johnny had guessed.

As Nameon was finishing his dance and the children waking from their trance SPLOT's first President and traitor came sneaking into the auditorium.

Tobias shook Benjamin back to his senses and pocketing the proceeds of the lottery they fled down towards the screen with a speed only fear can induce. Behind them legs stuck out on either side of the aisle like the closing of the Red Sea, and Johnny came tumbling down. It would have been difficult for the smaller children to keep him down had not Billy Owen, who was terribly glad that he had not been turned into a frog, decided to sit on him. This gave Benjamin time to drag Nameon, dizzy from his spinning, towards an exit, while Tobias collected the dwarf's clothes. They dressed him quickly and were several streets away from the cinema before a pale and frightened-looking Mr Fisher managed to untangle Johnny from the Lilliputians that clambered on top of him.

Outside, Johnny's pursuit of the children was further hampered by the people he had telephoned earlier and by neighbours from Micawber Street, all of whom were shouting for his blood. They were kept back only by the presence of two policemen who were also interested in Johnny. His phone-calls had caused havoc. The RSPCA van, after numerous breakdowns, had crashed into a van from the zoo, and as this was wrongly interpreted as malice by the RSPCA driver, a fight had ensued. When the television crews and journalists began entering Micawber Street someone leapt to the conclusion that a fire must have broken out and so eventually an ambulance and two fire-engines arrived on the scene. It was chaos. The only person Johnny had contacted who was not present was William D'Arcy. Having previous experience of Johnny's character, as soon as he saw the chaos he guessed what had happened and rushed back to his office to write the story of how a Steelborough youth had hoaxed the entire mass media, excluding himself, into believing he had trapped a leprechaun in his father's pigeon shed. The story was rushed into print and appeared not only in the local edition of the *National Evening News*, but also in the edition Mr Moon had used to wrap up Wanderlust. The headline had been:

LEPRECHAUN FOUND IN STEELBOROUGH
HOAX OR FACT?

26

In the back streets and alleyways behind the cinema Tobias and Benjamin hid Nameon as best they could. But it would have been easier hiding from a dozen policemen than from Johnny. He knew the area as well as his younger brother, and there were few hiding places in which the fugitives felt even remotely safe. The demolition sites and the derelict gardens, the back alleys, the rag-and-bone yards and the coal-piles behind the gasworks, these and all the other secret places where the local children hid from make-believe enemies were now used in earnest. They seemed impoverished places to Nameon, but it took only a little imagination for Tobias and Benjamin to transform them into kasbahs and futuristic cities.

In an area that had been prepared for demolition for as long as Tobias could remember but that had never actually been pulled down were two particularly long streets, called, ironically, Primrose Walk and Wavertree Vale, and between them was an alley bricked up at both ends. It was the one hiding place completely unknown to Johnny for it had come into being about the time he had decided games of hide-and-seek were beneath him and had moved to the superior pastime of pilfering telephone-boxes.

From the street the alley was inaccessible, but by squeezing through one of the boarded-up doors in Wavertree Vale it was possible for them to enter the house, pick their way across the decaying floors and emerge into the back. This they had done, and for a good half-hour had sat whispering together. 'We call these houses DKs,' said Tobias proudly. 'They're more interesting than parks. You find things like old threepenny bits.'

They believed the alley the perfect hiding place and might have stayed there hours had not the gradual accumulation of cats frightened Nameon. They prowled the walls with such stealth and confidence he could not help but think the alley their natural environment, and one which they could defend with the ominous claws they so frequently displayed. Not even Tobias' futile attempt to catch one of the cats could convince Nameon they were harmless and soon another, catless, hiding place had to be found.

Before it grew dark the children took Nameon to the railway station and with the collection money from the cinema Benjamin Platts bought the necessary ticket while Tobias and the dwarf waited in a corner by the left-luggage office.

When Nameon was given the ticket he thought some mistake had been made. The ticket looked unimpressive and hardly worth the trouble the children had gone through to get it. He had imagined something in the way of a large and dignified document, complete with ribbon and seal. In spite of all that had taken place since meeting the children, Norton Bay was still paramount in his mind. The way back was still a long way off.

To avoid any last-minute complications he insisted on finding the platform from which the 1.30 train would be leaving, and he memorized its whereabouts. There were several entrances to the station and the children showed him which would be the easiest to use, leading as it did out into streets near where they were hiding.

It was nearly five o'clock in the evening. In shop windows

lights were appearing. Benjamin and Tobias knew their mothers would soon be expecting them home, but with eight hours before the train departed they were reluctant to leave Nameon alone. They still sensed Johnny's presence among the streets, and whenever they moved one went on ahead to make sure Johnny could not take them by surprise. Thus the darkness when it came was welcome. In it they hunted for what Tobias called a safe base, a place near the station where Nameon could hide safely until his train departed. They settled for a playground in what had once been a private garden, but that now contained a few swings, monkey-ladders, and plenty of trees.

Tobias thought the playground too obvious a hiding place and one in which Johnny was bound to look, but when Nameon explained how dwarfs were capable of merging into any background that contained trees, he agreed.

It was after six when Benjamin left. His parting gift to Nameon was a brochure he had picked up in the travel office when he bought the ticket. Tobias envied the older boy's forethought, for the brochure was an advertisement for Norton Bay. It was brightly printed, the front showing a picture of a blue bay over which was superimposed a huge yellow sun. In large green letters at the bottom was the plea: 'Come to Sunny Norton Bay!'

'It won't actually look like that in winter,' said Benjamin, 'but the brochure might be useful.'

It looked very useful indeed. The brochure had been produced by the local council and was crammed with information and pictures of hotels and estuaries, as well as pictures of the bay itself. On the back was a map, less detailed than Nameon's, but similar enough to be recognized as a drawing of the same area.

Nameon gave the children his remaining three coins with instructions that one was to be given to someone called Billy

Owen. It was the one name Nameon had managed to take from the hat before being dragged out of the cinema. On hearing this Benjamin had burst out laughing and when Nameon and Tobias asked what was so amusing, he explained that Billy Owen had been the boy who mocked Nameon on the school-bus.

'Would you really have turned him into a frog?' he asked.

'Some things must remain secret,' said the dwarf with only the slightest hesitation.

Benjamin was nearly ten. It took him only moments to make up an excuse for why he had stayed out so late, but it took him nearly four years to make up enough excuses to convince himself that that Saturday had not happened exactly as he remembered it, and that the dwarf had probably not been what he had claimed to be. Within a year the coin he had been given was misplaced, and within two years it was lost for ever.

Tobias stayed with Nameon in the playground until his stock of excuses for staying out late no longer matched the time he was staying out. When he finally departed (much against his will and with a solemn shaking of hands) he exchanged addresses with the dwarf. Although he never expected them to meet a second time it made leaving easier.

A mist had descended over the streets, a mist that was like rain but was not rain. Nameon wandered the neighbourhood impatient for 1.30 to arrive. He kept close to the walls, passing countless houses in which televisions flickered and people sat, unconscious of the drama unfolding so near to them. He walked in no particular direction and was afraid to stand still for long, frightened that by loitering he would attract attention. Some corners smelt of fish and some corners smelt of tar and rain, or of nothing at all. On some corners stood groups of boys and girls, dressed smartly in their Saturday-night clothes, waiting for buses that would take them into town. The street lamps cast treacherous shadows, and in every shadow he imagined Johnny Plackham lurked.

The last time Nameon saw Johnny Plackham the boy was standing outside a public house, arguing with two friends. Nameon backed into an alleyway and watched, but then another, vaguely familiar shape passed near them and the boys separated.

When Nameon was sure his enemy had disappeared he felt a sense of loss as well as of relief. The streets suddenly seemed bleaker, and he thought that perhaps even an enemy was better than isolation, for now he was truly alone. The city had a harsh music of its own, a clanging and screeching that swelled and receded and was never quite the same. Only now that his attention was free did he hear it. Turning back down the streets Nameon relocated the playground and sat on a swing among the shadows to wait out the few remaining hours.

27

MR MOON arrived in Steelborough after spending more than four hours on the motorways that linked the cities. He immediately telephoned the *National Evening News* and asked for the address of the boy who had perpetuated the leprechaun hoax. It was after eight o'clock in the evening. William D'Arcy had long left work and when Mr Moon telephoned the only person left in the office was the charlady who informed him that the office was local and did not run a night staff. When he convinced her the address was a matter of life or death she leafed through D'Arcy's notebook and returned to the telephone with the information that the boy lived at 26 Micawber Street.

When Mr Moon arrived in Micawber Street he found the pavement outside No. 26 flooded with light. On the doorstep stood a tall, thin woman, presumably Mrs Plackham. She was shouting at a grubby-looking child and on either side of the road neighbours stood watching, as if the scene had been specially arranged for them. Eight bedroom windows were open and out of them hung thirteen children dressed in pyjamas. All were scrubbed pink and were listening intently to the conversation below.

Mr Moon parked within hearing distance and rolled down the car window. Wanderlust stuck his nose out into the evening, smelled excitement and without so much as a backward glance or a bark, leapt out of the car. Mr Moon neither noticed nor cared. He watched and listened, his attention riveted on the child.

The boy was rubbing an ear that seemed as if it might have received some attention from Mrs Plackham's hand. She was in fine fettle.

'Been watching a friend's television! You've been doing nothing of the kind, Tobias Plackham. You've been out in the streets all night, ashamed to come home. You know your father's pigeons have escaped? His pigeons!'

'Everything's Johnny's fault,' lamented the unfortunate youth. But the mother was not to be placated, and ordered the terrified child into the house. The boy rushed through the door like a mouse through a trap.

Inside the house the conversation was still audible, and from it Mr Moon deduced what had happened.

The rumour Johnny Plackham had spread about having a leprechaun locked in the pigeon shed had of course been true, and the younger boy had obviously rescued and probably only just left the dwarf. Which meant . . .

The skin on Mr Moon's face tightened. He realized in a city or a large town the world of a young boy can often be measured in streets rather than in neighbourhoods or miles. The dwarf was near, possibly only streets away.

Mr Moon left the car and began to walk. He wandered the streets in much the same manner as Nameon, but, although he never struck the right street, sometimes he was only separated from the dwarf by the thickness of a house.

Remembering how the dwarf had visited the Drowned Duck, Mr Moon searched the crowded bars as well as the empty streets, and he always had a drink before leaving. The alcohol bucked up his spirits, and rather than become dejected at not finding the dwarf, he began to feel more philosophical about it. Late in the evening on the corner of a street called Floral Street, behind which a gasworks loomed and in which a makeshift playground had been built, he came to another bar outside which three boys were standing arguing. In this particular pub an old man was playing an accordion and, coupled with Mr Moon's next drink, it was enough to alter his mood from carefree to melancholy.

When at eleven o'clock the public house closed Mr Moon was forced to sit on the steps outside, along with several other people who had become either too tipsy to walk or else had nowhere to go. He sat talking trivialities and attempting to clear his head. An hour later he discovered a fish-and-chip shop and bought the most excellent fishcakes he had ever tasted.

Shortly after one o'clock in the morning Mr Moon found himself back in Floral Street. The first time he had been in the street he had noticed a small playground. The gate had been closed and the swings still. Now the gate was open and one of the swings was moving, as if it had been bumped into or blown by the wind.

Mr Moon stood with his back to a wall facing the playground and in the gloomy enclosure he saw one shadow deeper than the rest. It was the dwarf, and it sat hunched against the trees sobbing.

Behind most windows the lights had vanished. It was near to freezing and Nameon was weeping with fatigue and self-pity. Discounting the lorry-cabin and the bus shelter, the last time he had slept properly had been in the porch of a country church accompanied by the tramp. His feet were blistered, his coat was soaked and heavy, and his thick, wide hands were numbed blue with cold.

He looked through the playground railings at the houses across the way and sensed by the stillness and darkness that it was time to move. He left the playground without examining the street, for he no longer expected Johnny to be hunting

him. In his coat pocket he fingered his ticket and maps. He crossed easily a road that hours ago had been alive with traffic, and at a set of traffic-lights turned into another road. Half-way down this was a narrow street called Station Walk, which led directly into the railway station. It was only then that Nameon became conscious of footsteps behind him and heard a slurred voice calling for him to stop.

At exactly twenty-nine-and-a-half minutes past one Mr Crosby, the ticket-collector, blew a whistle announcing the departure of the night train to Norton Bay and all places beyond. He hung his whistle back on its hook and was about to close the platform gate when two figures separated by no more than fifteen yards came hurtling towards him. Before he could say anything a grotesque-looking child, its face stained with tears and theatrical make-up, rushed past and tore along the platform towards the moving train. The child jumped, and, grabbing at a door-handle, pulled itself into the train. As it did so somebody whom the ticket-collector thought could only be the child's father pushed roughly through the ticket-barrier and clung dangerously to the door of the train's last carriage. Somehow he managed to open it and climb inside. The train clattered into the night. The ticket-collector had had no time to mention that the last carriage was a spare and that there were no connecting doors.

28

MR MOON fell back exhausted into the unlit carriage. He had left everything behind; his motor car, his case and all the personal documents and paraphernalia it contained. He did not care. He felt he no longer had any need for possessions. In his overcoat pocket was a half-full bottle of brandy bought the previous day in Lewsbury, and as the train drew out into the night he sat in the darkness, drinking.

The carriage window was like a black mirror and reflected in it was a face that no longer seemed to belong to him. It had grown thinner and paler, as if the years had passed over it in a matter of days. His limbs ached, and the pains in his chest had grown worse. He now viewed them as a normal part of his life. Briefly his mind flashed back to the doctor's surgery and to the note he had been given the day he first saw the dwarf.

In searching for Nameon he had done everything he ought not to have done and he was glad. He stood at the window swaying with the train's rhythm and he looked beyond his own reflection at the small lights that had become visible in the black fields outside. Behind each light, he thought, lived people who would never have such an adventure; who were doomed for ever to narrow rooms and narrow lives. He imagined his adventure remote from all other adventures. It was not an original thought but it moved him, and it seemed to him that no one had thought it before. He took another warming swig from the brandy bottle and flopped back into the upholstered seat. He wondered why the coach was not lit, and staggering out into the corridor another thought struck him: he did not know where the train was going. These thoughts seemed important for a moment, but then they evaporated, for it did not matter where he was going so long as he travelled with the dwarf.

When Nameon slammed the coach door and looked back to see who had been chasing him he had been astonished to discover it was not Johnny Plackham, but Mr Moon. The old man had managed to jump into the end carriage and although Nameon sat waiting for him to come through the connecting doors, no one appeared.

Mr Moon had ceased to exist for Nameon, and his persistence failed to impress the dwarf. Other things were more important. He dug into his pockets for the maps, and in the process discovered his one remaining apple. He ate it while studying them.

On his own map the crosses indicating the oak trees were at the tip of the northern extremity of the bay, a peninsula after which the land curved back on itself. His map set the two trees slightly apart from a group of symbols representing a pine forest. To the south of the forest Greenweed had drawn a tiny hamlet, cottages that were probably the origins of the present town. The Corporation map was similar in outline but concentrated on the whereabouts of the station, the town hall, the amusement arcades and the hotels, rather than on magic oak trees. Nameon was pleased to notice the station was north of the bay and thus near where he wanted to go. It all seemed far too easy, until he realized that no pine woods, in fact no trees at all, were indicated on the Corporation map. And then his pleasure vanished.

Hurriedly he scanned the printed information until he

read – *'The nature-lover will find Norton Bay the perfect place for a holiday. The lonely but refined stretch of coastland outside the town will suit perfectly his solitary moods. In the sixteenth and early seventeenth centuries the northern part of the bay was covered with pine woods but during the following century extensive flooding killed the trees, leaving only two giant oaks standing at the tip of the peninsula. Shortly after the beginning of the twentieth century these lone and majestic survivors were felled.'*

Nameon stared numbly at the words, and then read them again. He believed what they said, but fighting back panic he convinced himself that the stumps of the oak trees would still be visible and that these, along with the buried roots, would contain enough magic to work for him as they had for Greenweed. He clung to this last possibility for the remainder of the journey.

29

AFTER many hesitations the train finally arrived on the outskirts of Norton Bay. Nameon stood in the corridor with the windows pulled down. The air was dark and smelt of salt and rain. They were on high ground and he could make out the outlines of cliffs and beyond and below them the sea. The only sound was the baaing of sheep, for the gulls had not yet woken. The train moved at a snail's pace but soon the town with its wide bay, its bow-fronted hotels and its elegant houses came into view. The promenade followed the curve of the bay, and in front of it were gardens which in summer were full of flowering shrubs and fountains lit by coloured lights. But now in winter everything looked bleak. Light rolled in from the sea, as if brought on the waves. It spilt on to the rain-pocketed sand, illuminating the shuttered and weather-worn stalls and boat-houses. The train crawled to the edge of the town passing the sea front and stopping at a small, nondescript station.

The jerking of the carriages woke Mr Moon from the groggy sleep into which he had fallen soon after discovering he was cut off from the rest of the train. He opened a window and stuck his face out into what was still the night. There was no sign of the dwarf on the platform, but a carriage door farther along the train had been opened.

Mr Moon rushed along the platform. On a seat in the open carriage was a crumpled brochure and an apple core, nothing else. He ran the whole length of the train looking into windows. In one carriage sat an old couple, their heads resting on makeshift pillows, in another a soldier in a green uniform was yawning, and in yet another five musicians sat snoring in unison. There were other passengers and those who were awake returned his scrutiny with vacant stares.

Nameon was squeezing himself through the platform railings when Mr Moon finally saw him.

The station faced an expanse of flat marshy ground littered with hidden streams and interspersed by sand-dunes covered thinly by long yellow grass. Beyond them was the bay, only just now being touched by the sun. In the grass small birds cheeped miserably and moths clung to the separate blades shivering.

Nameon picked his way across tiny gullies and bogs, his attention riveted to the ground in front of him. He ignored the old man who followed behind him pestering him to stop. He felt neither the coldness nor the drizzle. Mr Moon's voice meant no more to him than the cry of the waking gulls.

Nameon found no evidence of the oak trees, no roots, no stumps, no scars; he found nothing. He crawled about, staring at the ground. He walked in crisscrosses and in circles, and so intent was his search that he began to recognize the shapes of stones he had already scrutinized. Mr Moon sat on a dune behind him, wheezing and wondering why the dwarf had travelled so far only to arrive at this small bleak peninsula with nothing to recommend it but solitude.

At the back of Nameon's mind a thought was trying to take form; it was as if he were a child on the verge of speech, with something important to say but unable to voice it. He refused to believe that nothing remained of the trees. Somewhere he thought, somewhere in one form or another they and their power must still exist. A little magic, enough to take me back. Eventually he lifted his eyes from the ground and when the after-image of grass and pebbles faded he scanned the bay.

Then the thought that had been evading him crystallized and with a cry of delight he leapt across the remaining sand-dunes and stumbled down on to the wrinkled beach. Startled by the dwarf's sudden movement Mr Moon rose awkwardly to his feet and followed.

The dwarf had flung off his overcoat and was running towards the wreck of an ancient fishing smack tilted on its starboard side well below the tide-line of scum and seaweed. He splashed through puddles, and flocks of indignant gulls rose in front of him. Mr Moon hobbled far behind, and soon the dwarf had disappeared into the skeleton of the wreck. When Mr Moon arrived he was astonished to find no trace of the dwarf. The dwarf, or leprechaun, or whatever it had been, had vanished. In all directions the landscape was empty. The wet sand contained only those footprints leading towards the boat. The terns and gulls had resettled in a mass of white, undisturbed dots. Bewildered, Mr Moon examined the inside of the boat. Into the wreck's oaken beams were carved the names and initials of people who had wandered inside it since it was stranded. Among the initials carved deeply into the side of the remains of a lifeboat was one name older and odder-looking than the rest. Mr Moon thought it was perhaps the name of the boat, or of a town, and he stared at it, puzzled as to why it held his attention. He pronounced the word out loud. 'Nameon,' he said, 'Nameon.' The word sounded strange to him.

He had come to some kind of end. He was ill and tired, and the hunt for the dwarf seemed suddenly far behind him and a long time ago. He felt too weak to think of how the dwarf had vanished or to make his way back across the sand to the town. Wondering where was the best place to rest, he found his attention drawn back to the lifeboat. He climbed into it, and curling up into a ball Mr Moon fell asleep.